WHAT
MY
GIRLFRIEND
DOESN'T
KNOW

ALSO BY
SONYA SONES

*What My Mother
Doesn't Know*

*One of Those Hideous Books
Where the Mother Dies*

WHAT MY GIRLFRIEND DOESN'T KNOW

sonya sones

SIMON & SCHUSTER BFYR

New York London Toronto Sydney

SIMON & SCHUSTER BFYR

An imprint of Simon & Schuster Children's Publishing Division
1230 Avenue of the Americas, New York, New York 10020
This book is a work of fiction. Any references to historical events,
real people, or real locales are used fictitiously. Other names,
characters, places, and incidents are products of the author's
imagination, and any resemblance to actual events or locales
or persons, living or dead, is entirely coincidental.
Copyright © 2007 by Sonya Sones
All rights reserved, including the right of
reproduction in whole or in part in any form.
SIMON & SCHUSTER BFYR is a trademark of Simon & Schuster, Inc.
For information about special discounts for bulk purchases, please
contact Simon & Schuster Special Sales at 1-866-506-1949
or business@simonandschuster.com.
The Simon & Schuster Speakers Bureau can bring authors to your
live event. For more information or to book an event, contact the Simon
& Schuster Speakers Bureau at 1-866-248-3049 or visit our website at
www.simonspeakers.com.
Also available in a SIMON & SCHUSTER BFYR hardcover edition.
Book design by Jennifer Reyes
The text for this book is set in Oranda BT.
Manufactured in the United States of America
First paperback edition December 2008
8 10 9
The Library of Congress has cataloged the hardcover edition as follows:
Sones, Sonya
What my girlfriend doesn't know / Sonya Sones.
p. cm.
Sequel to: What my mother doesn't know.
Summary: Fourteen-year-old Robin Murphy is so unpopular at high
school that his name is slang for "loser," and so when he begins dating
the beautiful and popular Sophie, her reputation plummets, but he
finds acceptance as a student in a drawing class at Harvard.
ISBN: 978-0-689-87602-8 (hc)
[1. Popularity—Fiction. 2. Self-esteem—Fiction. 3. Dating (Social
customs)—Fiction. 4. High schools—Fiction. 5. Schools—Fiction.
6. Artists—Fiction. 7 Novels in verse. 8. Boston (Mass.)—Fiction.]
I. Title. II. Title: What my girlfriend doesn't know.
PZ7.5.S66Wha 2007
[Fic]—dc22
2006014682
ISBN: 978-0-689-87603-5 (pbk)

For Poppy—
crusty, courageous, and cute

Acknowledgments

Infinite thanks to all the people who wrote and told me that they just *had* to know what happened next; and to Myra Cohn Livingston, for setting me on the path; Steven Malk, for holding my hand; Betsy Hochberg, for guiding my tour; Ron Koertge and Richard Peck, for talking story; Rose Brock, for listening; Alexis and Michael Sones, for the sunset shoot; Jack Floyd, for his website wizardry; David Gale, for his patience; Mike Esposito, for his footshake; David Schoffman, for his eloquence; Bennett, for his constant pep talks; Ava and Jeremy, for sharing me with Mr. Inspiron; and to the ladies of the pink kitchen—Ann Wagner, Betsy Rosenthal, April Halprin Wayland, Peg Leavitt, and Ruth Lercher Bornstein—for their unwavering wonderfulness.

And, of course, to the *real* Murphy, wherever he is. . . .

A Piece of Advice from Me to Me

Better brace yourself,
loser.

Because you
are about to be dumped.

Big time.

But It'll All Be Over in a Minute

All
be over
and done with.

Sophie's just standing there
staring at me
from across the cafeteria.

Geez.
Look at her.
Have you ever seen anyone so beautiful
in your life?

How could a girl like her
ever have wanted
to be with a guy like me?
Even just for two weeks?

Grace is waving her over.
Rachel's calling her.
"Fifi. Hey, Fee, we're over here!"

But *I'm* calling her, too.
Calling her with my eyes.
Come to me, Sophie.

Come to *me* . . .

Aw, Man

Who am I kidding?
I know exactly
what she's gonna do.

A second from now
she'll yank those killer blue eyes of hers
away from mine

and walk straight over to Rachel and Grace.
Like I'm not even here.
Like the best two weeks of my life

never

    even

        happened.

But They *Did* Happen

With everyone gone for winter break,
Sophie and I were
the only two people on the planet.

It was sort of like we were inside
one of those little snow globes,
you know?

Just the two of us,
completely alone,
chilling under that thick glass dome—

skating
and drawing and dancing
and kissing . . .

And I practically went into shock
when Sophie looked straight into my eyes
and told me she loved me.

Even if I come down
with a severe case of amnesia,
I'll never forget *those* two weeks.

And I'll Never Forget Those Kisses, Either

Because
making out with Sophie
was a *very* big deal for me.

See,
I'm not exactly what you'd call
the most experienced guy in the world.

Okay.
So I'm the *least* experienced guy
in the world.

Okay.
So Sophie was the first girl
I ever laid lips on.

But it was *definitely*
worth waiting
fourteen years for.

Even So

I told her I'd understand if it has to end.
And *sure* I'll understand.
Because, I mean, what girl in her right mind
would want to be seen hanging with *me*?

With *Murphy*, for chrissake,
the ugliest guy at Cambridge High?
The guy whose last name people use as a diss.
As in: "You are a real Murphy."

Let's face it.
I'm the type of guy
who doesn't even have any buddies
on my buddy list.

So I'll understand all right.
But this feels way worse than I thought it would, even.
Like my neck's on the chopping block
and the guillotine's getting ready to fall.

Because when I was *with* her, I was Robin.
Robin Murphy.
The guy who Sophie Stein loved.
The guy who made her laugh.

With*out* her,
I'll just be Murphy again—
Murphy the Lowly,
the guy who makes everyone *else* laugh.

But for all the wrong reasons.

Which Will Truly Suck

Because I've been Robin
for two whole weeks now.
Two life-alteringly awesome weeks.

And take it from me—
the grass actually *is* greener
in the other guy's yard.

So I don't think I'll be able to handle it
if I have to go back
to being Murphy again.

Though that's
what's about to happen,
whether I like it or not.

Just as soon as Sophie walks over there
to sit with Rachel and Grace
and pretends like she doesn't even know who I—

Whoa . . .
Whoa!
Whoa!

Sophie's heading straight toward *me*!

It's *Me* She's Racing Over To

Me!

Not Rachel and Grace.
Me!

It's me she's sitting down with.
Me she chose.

And she doesn't seem to care
if the whole school knows.

Is this really happening?
How can this be?

I feel like I've just won
the lottery!

Sophie Takes Hold of My Hands

Right
in front
of everyone—
sending supersonic shockwaves all through me.

And we just sit here,
grinning at each other like Muppets,
knees pressed together under the table,
eyes locked . . .

Until the bell rings.
"Check, please," I call,
snapping my fingers at an imaginary waiter.
This makes Sophie laugh.

And the sound of that laugh,
and knowing that *I'm* the one who made it happen,
makes me feel sort of all-powerful,
indestructible,

immortal, even.

So What Happens Now?

I'll tell you what happens.

Rachel and Grace creep toward us,
clutching each other's arms
like they're approaching an open coffin—

Grace's eyes bigger than DVDs,
Rachel's mouth hanging open so wide
you could reach right in and perform a tonsillectomy.

"Fee," Grace hisses
through teeth clenched tighter than lockjaw,
"*what* are you doing?"

When Sophie looks up at them,
her smile disappears,
and suddenly I feel like a man overboard.

Like
if she lets go of my fingers,
I'll drown.

But She Just Squeezes Them Even Tighter

While her eyes
dart back and forth
between her friends and me
like a pair of crazed hummingbirds.

"What does it look like I'm doing?"
she finally says.
"It looks like you're going psycho on us,"
Rachel says, with a nervous giggle.

"Well, she's not," I hear myself say
in this surprisingly friendly voice.
"Sophie's totally sane . . .
and totally amazing."

At which point,
that brilliant smile of hers
blazes back on like a torch,
and I can feel my heart catching fire.

"Oh, I'm sorry," Sophie says, all nonchalant.
"I guess I forgot to introduce you guys.
Rachel,
Grace—

I'd like you to meet Robin."

"Robin?!"

They gasp in unison.
"But . . . but . . ." Grace sputters,
"this . . . this is *Murphy!*"

"*Robin* Murphy," I say,
holding out my hand for her to shake.
"Any friend of Sophie's is a friend of mine."

But she backs away from me
like I have leprosy or something,
pulling Rachel right along with her.

Rachel manages a shell-shocked smile
and mumbles, "Uh . . . nice meeting you."
Then both of them turn and bolt from the cafeteria.

Sophie and I
just sit here in silence,
watching them go.

Then she says, "Well.
I'm glad *that's* over with."
But she doesn't look too glad to me.

And Neither Does Anyone Else

As Sophie and I walk through the halls,
holding hands on our way to art class,
it feels like we're committing a crime.

Everyone who sees us
looks offended, grossed out,
horrified, even,

as though I'm King Kong,
and Sophie's the little blonde
struggling to escape from my huge hairy fist.

They're gawking at us,
like Sophie's Beauty and I'm the Beast.
Like I'm Shrek and Sophie's Fiona.

I can feel her palm
beginning to sweat in mine.
I can feel her fingers stiffening.

But when I try to let go of her hand,
so that people won't know
we're together—

she won't let me.

Instead

She tugs me into this little alcove
where the custodian stows his brooms.

Then she presses her forehead against mine
and traces a heart on my palm
with the tip of her forefinger.

"There's something
so great about this," she whispers.
"About what?" I whisper back.

"About *this*," she whispers.
"About being outlaws.
It's just you and me—against the world."

Now do you get
why I like her so much?

I'm a Hundred Percent Hers

I mean, if I had to choose right now
between a single kiss from Sophie

or, say,
being the only guy at a week-long orgy
with all of the models
from the Victoria's Secret catalog,

I'd choose that single kiss.
Honest.

Okay.
I can guess what you're thinking.

You're thinking
my brain must have turned to mush
from all those years
I spent in social solitary confinement.

You're thinking
I'm a hopelessly romantic idiot.

And you know what?
You're right.

So I Make Sure No One Can See Us

Then I pull her to me and I kiss her.
I kiss her like my life depends on it.
And the scary thing is—it *does*.

Then I take her hand,
and we head back out into the hall,
surfing on a wave of us-against-them.

I feel exhilarated, brave,
invincible, even.
For about a minute.

But things seem to be escalating.
Now everyone who sees us together
does this shrinking-away-from-us thing,

like Sophie and I
have a bad case of lice.
Or maybe a touch of the plague.

When We Round the Next Corner

We see Dylan,
Sophie's irritatingly good-looking ex.
And when he spots Sophie and me holding hands,
he freezes, like he's been zapped by a stun gun.

Then he starts snickering
and shaking his head.
"That's wicked funny, Sophie.
Boy, you sure had me *going* there for a second . . ."

So.
He thinks he's been punked, does he?
He thinks the idea of Sophie and me being together
is some kind of laugh riot?

I'll show that scumbag.
I'll show him.
But first,
I better check with Sophie.

I whisper my idea to her
and she tells me to go for it.
So I do—
I give her a great big juicy kiss.

And when we finally pull apart
and brush past Dylan,
to head down the hall to Schultz's room,
his face looks whiter than Elmer's Glue.

A Minute Later

When Sophie and I walk into art class,
we're giving each other props,
feeling pretty good,
pretty triumphant, even.

But when people see us
laughing together
and holding hands,
the room goes morgue quiet.

And
all of a sudden,
my chest feels like
it's caving in.

Sophie lets go of my hand to head to her desk.
But just before she gets there,
Zak Benson flings himself down on his knees
right in front of her.

Then he puts his hands together
like he's praying.
"Tell me it ain't so!" he begs.
And everyone in the room starts snickering.

Sophie just shakes her head
and slips into her chair,
like she can't be bothered
with this half-wit.

But even from across the room,
I can see her nails turning white

where she's gripping her desk,
see her face going paler than the moon's.

She looks over at me
and shoots me a smile.
But I can see what's hidden behind her eyes.
And my heart almost flatlines.

Mr. Schultz Says He Wants Us to Draw a Feeling

A *feeling*?
Give me a break.

Art's my favorite class.
And Schultz's assignments are usually cool.
But I'm in no mood for *this* one.

So I just sit here for a while,
watching Sophie pretend
to be all involved in what she's drawing,

watching her be so careful
not to let what's churning in her gut
show on the outside.

Then I choose a stick of charcoal
and start sketching a girl
with dark smudges where her eyes should be.

I use an oil pastel
to make a deep red gash
where her heart should be.

Next, I draw a ball and chain
locked to the girl's ankle.
And then I add the final touch:

a shadowy face on the ball—
mine.

We Don't Have Any Other Classes Together

But between History and English,
I catch a glimpse of Sophie's back
up ahead of me in the corridor,
weaving through the stampede of students.

She's walking by herself.

Which really gets to me.
Because before today,
she always moved in a pack,
with Rachel and Grace
and Zak and Danny and Henry.

Now, she's alone.

And all around her, people are smirking
and whispering and nudging each other.
I have to fight the urge
to run and catch up with her
and shout at all of them to just CUT IT OUT!

That would only make things worse.

Because Sophie may *feel* like an outlaw,
but thanks to yours truly,
what she *really* is
is an out*cast*.

It takes one to know one.

After School

I'm blowing on my fingers
to keep them from freezing,
waiting for Sophie at the appointed spot—
by the goalpost
at the far end of the football field.

I'm trying not to think about anything.
Especially not about
how I'm wrecking Sophie's life.

It's ridiculous how much I've missed her.
We've only been apart for two hours,
but it feels more like two weeks . . .

Whoa!
Here she comes now,
flying toward me like a perfect fifty-yard pass,

her brown hair billowing out behind her,
her eyes reflecting the January sky,
her long skirt hugging her legs—

those incredible legs of hers,
that are carrying her closer and closer to me
with every step,
legs that'll be pressing up against mine
just a few seconds from now . . .

I used to think
it was only *girls*
who got weak in the knees.

Sophie Hurtles into My Arms

And suddenly I feel
like I've just scored the winning touchdown.

She wraps herself around me,
resting her cheek against my chest.

And the feel of her against me,
the smell of her hair,

thaws every atom
of my frostbitten body

and makes my heart reach warp speed so fast
that I almost keel over.

There are so many things I want to say to her.
But all of them are way too lame.

So I don't say anything.
I just kiss her . . .

And the cheering crowd
lifts me up onto its shoulders

and carries me away.

When We Finally Come Up for Air

Sophie's eyes
are smiling into mine.

And it's amazing, really,
because all she has to do is look at me

and my lump of a nose
straightens out,

the muscles on my arms
start to sprout,

the circles fade
under my eyes,

my ears shrink down
to a normal person's size . . .

If only everyone else
could see

what Sophie sees
when she looks at me.

She Tells Me Not to Worry

"Everything will be all right," she says.
"They'll get used to the idea of us being together.
This'll all blow over.
It *will*."

Then she says what she always says—
"Sometimes I just *know* things."
And I sure hope she's right about *this* thing.
Because if she's wrong, we're screwed.

"Come on," she says. "You're gonna walk me home."
"But what if we run into someone you know?"
"What *if*."
And she leans in for one last kiss.

Then she punches her fist in the air,
shouting, "Outlaws rule!"
And when she turns and sprints toward Broadway,
I chase after her,

feeling like the luckiest desperado alive.

Then—*THWOMP!*

A snowball explodes
between my shoulder blades,

rock hard
and seething with ice.

It's a snowball
that means business.

A snowball
with a message.

A message that's coming in
loud and clear.

But when we whirl around to see who delivered it—
nobody's there.

Though I could swear
I hear the wind whispering,

"What a Murphy . . .
Murphy . . . Murphy . . ."

Sophie Rubs My Back

"You okay?" she asks.

And that's when I notice
that her face has gone whiter
than the snow,

that her lips
are a thin, straight line,
and her eyes are blinking back tears.

So I pull myself together
and do my best stoner impression:
"Whoa . . . dude," I say. "That was *cold*."

And when Sophie laughs at my pun,
the ache between my shoulders
disappears.

Then We Get on a Roll

And start punning like crazy,
cracking each other up
as we make our way toward her house.

"Man," she says.
"Talk about trying
to *freeze* someone out."

"I've heard of giving people
the *cold shoulder*," I say,
"but this is ridiculous."

"Why can't they just accept the fact
that they don't have a *snowball's* chance in hell
of breaking us up?" Sophie says between giggles.

And when we get to the corner,
we don't even hesitate—
we turn onto Quincy instead of going straight.

Neither one of us mentions it,
but both of us know that if we use *this* route,
we probably won't bump into Rachel and Grace.

So what
if it'll take us ten minutes longer
to get to Sophie's house this way?

When We Step Inside Her Front Door

We hear the theme song
from *Days of Our Lives*,
just sort of hanging there in the air
like a layer of smog.

Sophie glances up the steps
and seems to sag a little,
like she's just put on one of those heavy padded vests
that they make you wear when they x-ray your teeth.

She calls out, "Hi, Mom. I'm home."
And then she adds, "Robin's with me,"
in a voice that sounds like what she *really* means is,
"So don't come down here—whatever you do."

Mrs. Stein calls down a muffled hello
as Sophie grabs my hand
and pulls me into the kitchen,
kicking the door shut behind us.

I fiddle with the knobs on the radio till I find K-ROK,
the station that plays all the best golden oldies.
Then I start singing along with the Righteous Brothers,
telling Sophie she's lost that lovin' feeling.

"No I haven't," she says.
And she pulls me to her for a kiss—
one of those incredibly deep soul-type kisses,
that switches off my brain

and switches *on* the whole entire rest of me . . .

But a Second Later

Sophie's mom shoves open the door!

She just stands there, blinking at us.
Like maybe she's seen a ghost—
a ghost that's been kissing her daughter!

I've never been caught
making out with a girl before,
so I'm not really sure what I'm supposed to do.

Apologize?
Act like it didn't happen?
Run like the wind?

I don't know who's
turning redder,
me or Mrs. Stein.

She keeps opening her mouth and closing it again,
like she really wants to say something,
only she doesn't know exactly what.

Finally,
she clears her throat.
Then she clears it again.

Then
she clears it a third time
and says,

"Hi."

That's All She Says

Just "Hi."
And suddenly
I get this overwhelming urge
to bust out laughing.

But I swallow hard
and pull myself together.
"Hi, Mrs. Stein," I say. "How are you?"
"Fine," she says. "And you?"

"Oh, I'm *fine*, thank you," I say,
trying to sound kind of decent and upstanding
and like she didn't just catch me
in a lip-lock with her daughter.

Sophie,
on the other hand,
doesn't say anything to her mom.
But if looks could kill . . .

A Partial List of Mrs. Stein's Excuses
for Coming into the Kitchen Every Five Minutes
After That to Spy on Us

- she needs to put the roast in the oven
- she needs some bottled water from the fridge
- she needs to add Post-its to the shopping list
- she needs to recycle the junk mail
- she needs to check on that roast
- she needs to search for some toothpicks
- she needs a sheet of paper and a pen
- she needs an envelope and a stamp
- she needs to check on that roast again
- she needs to get the laundry out of the dryer
- she needs the iron and the ironing board
- she needs to make sure that we aren't having sex
- she needs to check on that roast again

But In Between All of Her Mom's Interruptions

Sophie and I
still manage to engage in
some pretty serious footsies
while we do our homework.

Then we start playing that game where one person
draws a random squiggle on a sheet of paper
and the other person
has to turn that squiggle *into* something.

Which is when K-ROK starts blasting out
Ray Davies singing "You Really Got Me."
That's when I notice that Sophie's squiggle
sort of *looks* like Ray Davies.

So I tell her I'm gonna turn it into a portrait of him.
"Who's Ray Davies?" she asks.
And while I draw him,
I tell her all about him—

about how he was
the lead singer of the Kinks,
this amazing British rock group
from the sixties.

I tell her
the name of every song Davies ever wrote,
who performed it,
and what instruments they played.

And when I finish, Sophie just stares at me
in this real I-don't-*believe*-this kind of way,

and says, "But I bet you can't tell me
where they *bought* those instruments."

"Well, actually," I say,
"I think they got them from this store called—"
But Sophie puts her finger to my lips.
"Robin," she says, flashing me a heart-stopping grin.

"I was *kidding.*"

Then She Asks Me

How come I know so much
about prehistoric rock and roll.
And I explain that it's because my parents
turned me on to it when I was like zero years old.

I mean, my dad used to play
his Beach Boys records for me
when I was still swimming around in the womb,
for chrissake.

And after I was born,
instead of singing me "Rock-a-Bye Baby,"
my mom used to sing "Baby, I Love You,"
this awesome old song by the Ronettes.

My parents didn't read to me
from Mother Goose.
They turned me on
to the Mothers of Invention.

I grew up knowing more
about Dr. John the Night Tripper,
than I did about Dr. Seuss.
"I didn't bother collecting bugs . . ." I tell her.

". . . I had the Beatles!"

"*And* Ray Davies," Sophie Says

Then she grabs my pencil
and starts drawing a picture
of this happy little guy jumping for joy.

"Who's that?" I ask.
"It's *Hooray* Davies," Sophie says.
Which cracks me up.

So then I draw this dude
spinning around inside a blender.
"Say hello to *Pureed* Davies," I say.

Which cracks *her* up.
And we spend the rest of the afternoon like this—
drawing funny pictures for each other.

We draw Toupee Davies,
Valet Davies, Partay Davies,
Betrayed, Dismayed, and Tooth-Decayed Davies.

And when we finish, Sophie says,
"That was the most fun I've ever had drawing
in my entire life."

I love having an artist for a girlfriend.

It's Time to Go

But it's hard to say good-bye to Sophie.

And downright impossible to *kiss* her good-bye,
what with her mother lurking, silent but deadly,
just a few feet away from us in the hallway,
giving me the evil eye . . .

You know, on second glance,
Sophie's mom doesn't look *that* unfriendly.
In fact, I could have sworn
she just cracked a smile at me.

It couldn't be because she likes me, though.
It's probably because I'm finally leaving—
and with her daughter's virginity
still intact!

But I wouldn't be
so sure of that if I were her.
There *was* that one six-and-a-half-minute stretch
when she forgot to check on us . . .

 (I'm just playin' wit' ya.)

On the Walk Home

I'm watching the sun
paint the snowdrifts pink,

my grin so wide
it practically won't fit on my face,

still floating
from my afternoon with Sophie,

feeling like someone who's fun to be with,
like someone who's cool,

someone who's funny,
someone who's got a girlfriend,

someone who's *worthy*
of having a girlfriend, even . . .

just floating along
feeling like

*some*one.

As I Pass by the Playground

Of my old elementary school,
I happen to notice
a couple of little kids
zipping around on the ice rink.

I watch as the girl skates up behind the boy,
yanks off his hat and whizzes away with it,
making him lose his balance
and crash down hard on his butt.

The boy doesn't even try to get up.
He just sits there and starts crying.
The girl looks guilty at first.
Then she slams her mittens onto her hips.

"Geez," she says
as she skates back over to him
and starts pulling him up by his sleeve.
"Don't be such a *Murphy*."

And when I hear her say this,
I feel like I've been kicked,
real hard,
in the stomach.

"Don't Be Such a Murphy"

It was Fletcher Boole who coined that phrase.
Not long after I moved here
in the middle of fourth grade.

I was such a clueless little goofball back then
that it took me forever to figure out
that he was using "Murphy" as an insult.

But when I finally *did*,
I started lying awake at night,
inventing new last names for myself:

Robin Greightguy.
Robin Nycekidd.
Robin Neetboi.

So that if Fletcher or anyone else
ever tried to use my name
to diss someone again,

they'd end up having to say something like,
"Whoa, man . . .
you are such a Kewldood!"

Kept myself entertained for hours that way.

But I'm Not Feeling Particularly Entertained at the Moment

I'm trudging toward my house
with my fists jammed deep into my pockets,
trying to make sense out of what just happened.

I mean, I knew the Murphy-as-insult thing
had followed me to middle school.
And then, this fall, to high school.

But, until now,
I hadn't even considered the possibility
that I'd become a legend
in my own time.

That even after I *left* a place,
my name would live on behind me
like some kind of terrible echo.

That it would keep right on rolling off the tongues
of dozens of snot-nosed little twerps
who'd never even *met* me.
Elementary school kids, even.

Until now, it hadn't crossed my mind
that "Murphy" might have earned itself
a permanent spot in the dictionary.

Maybe
when I get home,
I'll look myself up.

I Crack Open the Front Door

And the first thing I hear
is the sound of Mom and Dad
singing along to a CD of Aretha Franklin.

It's that great song about how
all she wants is just a little respect . . .
Man oh man—I sure can relate to *that*.

Their voices are coming from the kitchen,
where from the garlicky smell of things
I figure they must be whipping up a spaghetti dinner.

I slip into the hall,
sneak past the kitchen door,
and slink up the stairs to my bedroom.

Because if there's one thing
I don't feel like doing at the moment,
it's baring my soul to the parental units.

And if they intercept me right now
and start asking me how school was,
I'll spill my guts for sure.

My parents are great listeners.
Which is why I never tell them
*any*thing.

Since Whenever I *Do*

They try to force-feed me all this lame advice
that *their* parents gave *them* when they were my age.
Which is such a joke.

Because I just don't see how two people
who were born almost forty years
before the new millennium

could think they have anything to say to me
that would have even the slightest bit of relevance
to life on planet Earth as we know it *now.*

Like when Fletcher
first started slinging my name around school
as though it was some kind of swear word—

Dad said it was because
Fletcher felt threatened by me,
since I was way smarter than him.

Mom said Fletcher was only doing it
to get a rise out of me,
and that he'd stop if I'd just ignore him.

"Trust us on this one," they said.
So I trusted them.
And what did it get me?

My very own entry in the dictionary.

Mur·phy (Mur'fē) *n., pl.*-phies. *Slang*

1. a. Loser. One who fails to win. At anything. Ever. **b.** One who sucks in quality; an inferior member of the human species: *That guy is a real Murphy.* **2.** A person regarded as stupid, inept, ridiculous, and/or butt-ugly. **3.** One who occupies the lowest possible rung on the food chain. **4. a.** A person deserving of scorn and ridicule. **b.** "Lowlier than thou." **5.** Geek. **6.** Dweeb. **7.** Schlemiel. **8.** Nerd. **9.** Jerk. **10.** Freak. (From the Greek *murphosis*, the process of forming or assuming the shape of a moron; from *murphoun*, to behave like a moron; from the Latin *robinus murphatus*; from *murphus*, *murphtum*, *murpha*, moron. See MORON.)

I'm Practically Inhaling My Dinner

Pretending I'm starving,
trying to avoid eye contact with my parents.
Because if they take a close look at me,
they'll see how messed up I feel right now.

And if they see how messed up I feel right now,
my dad'll cock his head to the side, the way he does,
and my mom'll do that thing
where she brushes the hair off my forehead.

And then they'll both just sit there staring at me
with this you-don't-have-to-tell-us-
but-we-sure-would-like-to-know-what's-bothering-you
kind of look in their eyes.

And if they start looking at me like *that*,
then all three of us know
that even if I try real hard *not* to,
I'll end up telling them everything.

And if I end up
telling them everything,
then chances are pretty good
I'll start crying.

And if I start crying,
I'll feel all weak and pathetic.
And *that*'ll make me feel even more messed up
than I was feeling in the first place.

So, I'm practically inhaling my dinner,

pretending I'm starving,
trying to avoid eye contact
with my parents.

But the only thing
I'm *really* starving for
is the sound
of Sophie's voice.

She Answers Her Cell on the First Ring

"Hey," I say.
"Hey, yourself."
"Whatcha doing?"
"Taking a bath."

Gulp.
"No kidding?"
"No kidding."
And she sloshes the water a little to prove it.

"Whoa . . ." I say,
". . . are there, like, bubbles involved?"
She giggles.
"Tons."

Suddenly, I can imagine her,
imagine every slippery inch of her—
which parts are poking out through the suds,
which parts are hidden.

And my body gets so overheated,
it almost sets the bed on fire.
"I wish I was there . . ." I say.
"You know, *with* you in there."

"I wish you were, too," she says.
"But that wouldn't go over real big with my mom."
"It wouldn't go over real big with *anybody*," I say.
"It would go over real big with *my* body," she says.

And we both crack up.
"Mine, too," I say.

"Then that's all that matters, right?" she says.
"Me and you, us being together, in the tub or out of it."

"Us being together," I say,
"no matter what anyone else thinks."
And, at least for right now,
I can believe that.

I Turn Out the Light Early

And try to fall asleep,
hoping for another one of my Sophie dreams,
for one of those real steamy ones,

where we start out kissing
but then we start doing
all these other things—

things I'd never even *think*
of asking her to do
in real life.

Well, that's not exactly true.
I think of asking her to do things like that
all the time.

Only I don't ever actually ask her to do them.
Because I wouldn't want her to get the impression
that I'm a sex-crazed maniac.

Even though I *am* a sex-crazed maniac.

But I Wouldn't Feel Right

About rushing Sophie into anything
or pressuring her to do stuff
before she's really ready to do it.

Besides,
what would I do
if she said yes?

I mean,
what if just like in the dream I had last night,
we started out kissing each other
and then I started pulling her T-shirt off?

And, I mean,
what if I started doing that
and Sophie didn't even ask me
to stop?

What if she just closed her eyes
and let me slip it right off over her head
and then I saw that she wasn't even wearing a—

Aw, man.
Now I'll *never* be able
to fall asleep . . .

Tuesday Morning

I'm in the school library,
trying to focus on finding the books I need
for this project I got stuck doing for health class
on STDs.

But it's impossible to concentrate,
because I keep on thinking about Sophie,
wondering how she's doing,
hoping she's all right . . .

Then—
I hear her voice!
It's coming from
the other side of the bookshelf.

"I was busy," Sophie's saying.
"Doing *what*?" I hear Grace say.
"Playing with your new *boy toy*?"
"Just busy," Sophie says.

Now I hear Rachel's voice: "Well, me and Grace
called you about a hundred times last night."
"You've *got* caller ID," Grace says.
"You *knew* it was us."

"Why didn't you pick up?" Rachel says.
"We were way worried about you."
"And we still *are*," Grace says.
"Friends don't let friends commit social suicide."

And when I hear these words,
my heart detonates in my chest.

Rachel Laughs Nervously

"So, what's going on, Fee?" she says.
"You aren't really, like, *with* him, are you?
I mean, I just can't cope with that concept."

"Neither can I," Grace says.
"I thought I was hallucinating when I saw you
run over to him in the cafeteria."

Grace makes a retching sound and bursts out laughing.
Then she adds, "But I wasn't hallucinating.
Was I, Mrs. *Murphy*?"

"No. You *weren't*," Sophie says,
her voice as sharp
as broken glass.

And a second later
I see her hurrying toward the exit,
swiping at the tears rolling down her cheeks.

"Jesus, Grace," Rachel hisses,
"that was cold."
Then she shouts, "Fee! Come back!"

But Sophie doesn't even glance over her shoulder.
She just shoves through the library door
like she'd rather be shoving Rachel and Grace.

I want to run after her.
I want to wrap my arms around her.
I want to tell her that everything will be okay.

But if I do,
she'll know I've been eavesdropping.
And, besides—

maybe everything *isn't* gonna be okay.
Maybe everything's
gonna totally suck.

When Lunchtime Rolls Around

I try to convince Sophie we should skip the cafeteria.
"Let's eat in Schultz's room today instead," I say.
"What's up with *that*?" she says.
And, right away, my cheeks ignite.

I can't tell her I listened in on her conversation.
So I just shrug and say,
"If Rachel and Grace keep seeing us together,
they'll dump you."

"Too late," she says, with a sad little smile.
"They already *have*."
"What?" I say, my blood icing in my veins.
"Actually," she says, "it was *me* who dumped *them*."

Then she tells me all about
this big fight she had with them,
about how they cornered her in the bathroom
right after English class,

at which point Grace basically told Sophie
that she had to choose between
going out with *me*
and hanging out with *them*.

"So," Sophie says,
"I told them it was a no-brainer,
walked out of the bathroom,
and that

was that."

The Rest of the Week at School

Is just more of the same old crappy same old.

I don't really feel like sharing
all the gory details of the sick stunt
that Zak and Danny pulled on Sophie and me
in the cafeteria on Wednesday.

And I don't particularly want to tell you
how many minutes it took me to stop moaning
after Dylan "accidentally" rammed his knee
into a certain part of my anatomy on Thursday.

Or exactly what it was that Henry said
to Sophie and me in the hall this morning.
But it's funny how flattering an insult can sound
when it's hurled at you in an English accent.

So please don't ask,
because I'd rather not try to describe the look
that Rachel and Grace got on their faces just now,
when they saw Sophie and me leaving school together.

Or the look that Sophie got on *her* face,
when she saw the look on *theirs*.
It's just more
of the same old crappy same old.

But Sophie and I Figure

That maybe,
if we can just keep laughing it off
whenever those jerks do stuff like that,

maybe
we can keep it from seeping in,
keep it from creeping under our skin.

Maybe,
if we can just laugh
instead of shattering,

we can somehow
keep all of it
from mattering.

I'm Not Sure Whose Idea It Is

But after school,
we end up over at Adrenaline Zone,
the video arcade down on Brattle Street.
Sophie heads straight for
the Whack-a-Whatever game
and force-feeds it a couple of quarters.

Then she grabs a mallet
and starts bopping
those gophers or moles
(or whatever those things are
that keep popping up)
on their masochistic little heads.

Sophie's going at it like Buffy on a rampage,
slamming those rodents down
so fast and so furious
that when the game's finally over
a hundred tickets
gush out of the slot at the front.

Then she turns to me, all breathless,
with her eyes shining brighter than high beams,
and a smile as big as a slice of the moon.
"Omigod. You have *got* to try that!" she says.
"It feels soooooo good!"
So I do.

And it *does*.

Saturday Afternoon at the Museum of Fine Arts

Sophie and I are celebrating
our three-week anniversary
by revisiting the spot
where we first really talked:

the wooden bench
in front of our favorite painting—
Le Bal à Bougival,
Renoir's life-size picture of a dancing couple.

We're sitting side by side, sketching it.
The man with the yellow hat
is leaning in to the woman in the long white dress,
his red beard almost touching her cheek.

"That man . . ." Sophie says. "He looks like
he can hardly bear not to be kissing that woman."
"I know exactly how he feels," I say.
And when the guard looks away, we sneak a kiss.

Then Sophie rests her head on my shoulder and says,
"I've always wondered what it would feel like
to kiss a guy with a beard . . ."
"No problem," I say. "I'll grow one for you."

Sophie raises an eyebrow. "You can *do* that already?"
"Sure," I say, in the deepest voice I can muster.
"I've been shaving every day since I was like five.
Give or take seven years."

"No kidding?

And you'd grow a beard just for me?"
"Sure. And I'll throw in a mustache, too."
"That rocks!" she says.

And for the first time since sixth grade,
when everyone started teasing me about it,
my fast-growing facial hair
actually seems like a *good* thing.

I Haven't Shaved for a Week

What can I say?

I sort of look like Brad Pitt
having a bad face day.

And, man oh man,
it's such a bitch—

no one told me
how much it would *itch*.

Though You Couldn't Really Call This Thing a Beard Yet

It's more like a five o'clock shadow
with benefits.
Because Sophie says
she loves it already.

And she keeps on kissing me
to see how it feels,
kissing me
and stroking my stubble with her fingers.

She says there's just something
so cave-mannish about it,
so bad-boy, so Hell's-Angelly,
that it really *gets* to her.

And she keeps oohing and aahing
about how it makes me look so much older—
like a real man of the world, she says,
or a pirate, even.

And she says there's something
incredibly hot about that.
So *I* say: Who cares if it's a little bit itchy?
It worked for Abraham Lincoln.

Maybe it'll work for me.

My STD Project Is Due Soon

Here are the "fun facts" I'm putting on my poster:

You get an STD when you have unprotected sex
with someone who's had unprotected sex
with someone else who's given them an STD.

Or when you have sex with someone who has an STD
who lies to you about being a virgin,
so you don't bother using protection.

Or when you have protected sex
with someone who has an STD,
but the condom breaks.

Or when you have
unprotected oral sex
with someone who has an STD.

Approximately 46 percent
of high school students in the U.S. have had sex.
And one in four of them has an STD.

So, if you look around your classroom
at the thirty people sitting there,
fourteen of them probably aren't virgins.

And of those fourteen,
3.5 of them have an STD.
But which 3.5 people are they?

And which one is the person with only *half* an STD?

My Beard's Completely Grown in Now

Which means it's finally stopped itching.

And even though the usual jerks at school
still tease me about it every day,
it's been way worth it.

Because Sophie says
she loves it even more *now*
than when it was first sprouting.

She says
she loves the color of it—
calls it "cinnamon red."

And she loves the feel of it—
like rubbing her cheek
against cashmere, she says.

But most of all,
she loves that I grew it just for her.
And *I* love that that's why she loves it.

And that when I look in the mirror,
I see a new me,
a different me,

a me reinvented.

After School on Tuesday

Sophie invites me over to her house.
"Are you sure your mother won't mind?" I say.

"My mother won't *know*.
And neither will my father.
They went to see a marriage counselor
and said they wouldn't be home till 4:30."

I pull out my cell phone to check the time.
It's only 3:20.
If Sophie and I hurry,
we'll have almost an hour alone together!

"Come on," I say.
"I'll race ya!"

The Whole Way Over to Sophie's House

I'm fantasizing about everything
I'm gonna do with her when we get there . . .
if she'll *let* me, that is.
Which she probably won't.

Not that I'm complaining
about the fact
that all Sophie wants to do so far
is kiss.

Well, okay.
I guess I *am* complaining, a *little*.
But it's not really *me* who's complaining.
It's my body.

My body's all like, "Geez.
Is she *ever* gonna let me get to second base?
How much longer am I gonna have to suffer?
I want *more* and I want it *NOW!*"

My mind knows this is greedy.
My mind knows this is messed up.
My mind knows this is just plain wrong.
But my body

has a mind of its own.

When We Get to Sophie's House

We rush straight upstairs to her room.

Then we start kissing.
And we kiss for a long time—
till I can feel Sophie's heart
beating crazy fast against mine,

feel her breasts
pressing against my chest . . .
so soft . . . so warm . . .
so . . . so . . .

And before I even realize what I'm doing,
my hands are slipping under her T-shirt,
sliding up her torso . . .
up . . . and up . . . and up . . .

but just before they reach their destination,
Sophie gets this look on her face—
this look that's begging me to stop.
So I force myself to slam on the brakes.

Because even though
I'm lusting after Sophie's breasts
in a huge way, in a major way,
in a throbbingly intense way—

I've got to face
the painful fact
that Sophie's still not ready
for that to happen.

I Knew This Day Would Come

I knew it the whole time I was researching
all the different types of STDs you can catch,
and all the things you can do to catch them,
and all the things you can do
to *keep* from catching them.

All that whole time,
I knew I'd eventually be standing
where I am right now:
in front of my entire health class,

with everyone looking at me
like I'm something they wish they could
scrape off the bottom of their shoe,

while I stand here talking to them
about leaky blisters, and oozing sores,
and genital *warts*, for chrissake.

The whole time I was doing
all the stupid idiotic research
for this stupid idiotic report,
I knew this day would come—

when I'd be standing here,
staring into the smirking faces of my classmates,
while they fire questions at me like spitballs.
Questions like the one that Henry just asked:
"How do you spell 'vaginal discharge'?"

A Few Minutes Before Art Class on Friday

Sophie and I walk into Schultz's room
and find him scrambling
to erase a huge picture off the board,
muttering to himself about what he's going to do
to the person who "drew this abomination."

It's clearly a caricature of yours truly:
ears bigger than tennis rackets,
raccoon circles under the eyes,
beard like a fur ball some cat spit up,
nose more crooked than Harry Potter's scar.

They've drawn me with one of my hands
crammed down the back of a girl's jeans,
and the other hand crammed down the front.
Schultz has already erased the girl's face,
though it's obvious whose face it must have been.

When he glances over his shoulder and sees us,
his face turns redder than a maraschino cherry.
But he just smiles at us and says, "Hey kiddos.
Grab a box of oil pastels and some newsprint.
I've got a terrific project planned for today."

He's acting like everything's fine,
but I can't help noticing
that he doesn't seem to be able
to look either one of us
in the eye.

And I Know Exactly How He Feels

I'm so freaked
by that picture on the board,
that I can't even bring myself to *glance* at Sophie.
Besides, I don't think I could stand to see the look
that's probably on her face right now.

So I just gather up
some pastels and newsprint,
then sit down at my desk and start doodling—
all these real pissed-off little pictures
of fists hitting chins and bats cracking skulls.

A little while later,
when the rest of the class arrives,
Schultz runs his hands through his long white hair
and tells us that today
he wants us to draw the mood we're in.

The *mood* we're in?
I rifle through my box of pastels,
choosing my colors carefully:
pus green, puke grey, crap brown,
and bloody-murder black.

When I Pass In My Drawing at the End of Class

Schultz studies it for a while,
nodding his head slowly up and down,
like a bobblehead
thinking deep thoughts.

Then he tells me
he's got this friend named Felix
who teaches a drawing class
at Harvard.

"Felix stopped by yesterday,
and when I showed him some of your work,
he was so impressed with it
that he offered to let you audit his class."

"Audit it . . . ?"
"That's when you take a class for no credit.
You just sort of sit in on it.
Unofficially."

Schultz says Felix really hopes I'll say yes
because he thinks I'd be
a real inspiration to his other students.
An inspiration? Me? Whoa . . .

He says the class meets
on Monday and Wednesday nights.
And that the first meeting's next Monday.
He says I can think about it and let him know.

But I don't *have* to think about it.

After Class

When I tell Sophie what Schultz said,
she throws her arms around me.
"Oh, Robin! That's so cool!"
"Yeah. I guess it is," I say, "but I wish Felix
had invited *you* into the class, too."

"I *am* a little envious . . ." she says.
"Okay—I'm a *lot* envious.
But that guy was *right* to choose you.
You're like in a whole other league.
I mean, you could be the next Renoir."

"Well, if your prediction comes true," I say,
looking into Sophie's soft blue eyes,
"I'll paint a thousand portraits of you.
And I'll hang them in galleries all over the world,
so everyone can see how beautiful you are."

When I say this, she blushes.
And *God*—
she looks so amazing when she does that.
"It *will* come true," she whispers. "It will.
Sometimes I just know things . . ."

Friday Night

Sophie called a minute ago.

Her voice sounded choked,
like she was trying hard not to cry.
She told me she was gonna have to
cancel our date.

We'd had this sort of special night planned,
in honor of my being asked into the class at Harvard.
We were gonna have dinner together at Pinocchio's
and then take a walk along the river.

But Sophie said her mother's forcing her to go
to this dumb family dinner, instead,
in honor of her great aunt's third cousin's
annual thirty-ninth birthday or something.

My heart crashed
straight down to my feet
when she told me,
like an elevator with its cable cut.

But I said I understood.
And that it was okay.
Even though I *don't* understand.
And it *isn't* okay.

Seems like
Mrs. Stein's new favorite hobby
is thinking up evil ways
to keep Sophie and me

apart.

On Saturday Morning

When Sophie's mom finally lets her out of the house,
we head straight over to the museum
to celebrate our five-week anniversary
by sitting on the wooden bench
in front of *Le Bal à Bougival*,
and sketching the painting of the dancing couple.

Then we just sort of wander around Harvard Square,
being in love and stuff.
I take Sophie into Second Coming,
my favorite oldies record store.
And she *tries* to look interested, she really does.
But I can tell that she thinks it's a big yawn.

So after a few minutes, I suggest we head over
to the Christ Church Thrift Shop
to see if there's anything buy-worthy.
The second we walk in the door,
Sophie spots an old yellow hat.
Her eyes widen as she sets it on my head.

"Omi*god*," she says.
"With this hat and your red beard,
you look exactly like the guy in *Le Bal à Bougival!*"
And I guess the idea of this must turn her on,
because she pulls me behind a bookcase
for a kiss so hot that it practically vaporizes me.

That settles it—I am *definitely* buying this sucker.

Monday Mostly Stinks

It doesn't really bother me
how Rachel and Grace flatten themselves
against their lockers when they see me passing by.
Like I'm this skunk getting ready to spray.
At least Sophie isn't there to see them do it.

But when I'm walking to English class
and Dylan snatches my new yellow hat off my head,
then yanks open a window and flings it outside,
and everyone else around us cheers,
I gotta admit—*that* gets to me.

I'd like to beat that guy to a pulp.
I really would.
I'd like to slam my fist
right into that disgustingly straight nose of his
and make it look a little bit more like mine.

But that ain't gonna happen.
Because, let's face it—
Dylan's on the wrestling team.
And I may be pissed,
but I'm *not* brain-dead.

So I just nail him with a look
that lets him know I think he's scum.
Then I sprint down the two flights of stairs,
run outside, grab my hat,
and race back up again.

But somehow, someday,
I'll find a way to make that jerk pay.

One Hour Before My First Drawing Class

Is Sophie right about my hat?
Does it make me look like that guy
in the painting?

Or does it just make me look
like a pathetic fourteen-year-old loser
trying to pass himself off as a college student?

Does my beard *really* make me look older,
like Sophie says?
Or does it just make me look homeless?

Do you think there's enough time
for me to get some plastic surgery
between now

and seven o'clock?

Mom Drives Me Over to Harvard
Ten Minutes Early

We pull up in front of the Carpenter Center.
"Oh, Robin," she says,
getting all wiggly-voiced and teary-eyed.
"This is going to be so fabulous for you."
"Thanks, Mom," I say. "See you at ten."

Then I leap out of the car as fast as I can,
so no one will see that my mother drove me.
Besides, she's got that look on her face,
like she's thinking about
doing something desperate—
maybe even like hugging me in public!

When she drives away,
I turn to look at the modern building,
taking in all the curved concrete walls
and the strange ramps reaching out of it
like arms trying to grab me
and yank me inside.

It looks so what-am-I-doing-here?,
so sore-thumbish, so entirely out of place
among all these ancient ivy-covered buildings,
that it kind of reminds me of a UFO.
Or of an alien.

Or of *me*, even.

At Five Minutes Till Seven

I walk up one of the ramps
into the Carpenter Center,
take the elevator to the fourth floor,
and follow the signs to Studio B.

But when I finally find the door,
the actual door to the actual studio
where the actual art class will be held,
my heart shifts into overdrive.

And no matter how hard I try,
I can't seem to work up the courage to push it open.
So I just stand here staring at it
like an idiot . . .

Until a girl's voice from behind me says,
"There are things known
and there are things unknown,
and in between are the doors."

I whip around and see a short girl
looking up at me through wire-rimmed glasses
from under a brushfire of curly red hair.
"Know who said that?" she asks.

"Jim Morrison," I say, "of the Doors."
"*Damn*," she says, flashing me a grin
as she whisks past me and shoves open the door.
"You're the only one who ever got that right."

I Thought There'd Be More People Here

But there's less than a dozen students,
sitting around on tall metal stools
in front of easels.

A few of them look up
when the girl and I come in.

Though even after
they see us walk to the front of the room
and sit down next to each other
on the only two empty stools,
they just turn back around
and go on talking among themselves—

like my being here
is the most normal thing in the world.

Like *I*
have just as much right to be here

as anyone.

Even So, I Feel Like I'm Crashing a Party

Like any second now,
one of these Harvard students
will realize I'm only a high-school freshman
and toss me out of here on my butt.

So I'm just sitting on this stool,
sort of crossing and uncrossing my arms,
trying to be all inconspicuous and nonchalant,

half expecting
to overhear one of these people
calling someone a Murphy, even,

when this old guy steps out of a supply closet
and heads to the front of the class,
slipping a charcoal pencil behind his triple-pierced ear.

He's as bald as a basketball and nearly as round,
wearing a T-shirt and jeans and a tie-dyed apron
with a thousand layers of paint speckled all over it.

When he notices me watching him,
he smiles
and tips an imaginary hat to me.

And somehow, when he does this,
it makes me feel . . . I don't know . . .
like I've come to the right place, I guess.
So I smile back

and tip my *real* hat to *him*.

The Old Guy Clears His Throat

And says, "I'm Professor Kolsnikovashian.
Say it with me now, people:
Kols - ni - ko - . . .
Oh, never mind.
Just call me Felix."

Then he asks us
to introduce ourselves to each other,
starting with the girl who's sitting next to me,
the one who quoted Jim Morrison
on the way in.

She tells us her name is Tallahassee,
but that we can call her Tessa.
The guy next to Tessa
introduces himself as Harrison.
But says he likes to be called Honk.

Then comes Susannah,
who asks us to call her Suze.
And Kennedy, who prefers Ned.
Then Jeremiah, who wants us to call him Jake.
And Katherine, who'd like to be known as Kat.

The girl next to Kat is Evelina,
but she goes by Eve.
And the girl next to Eve says, "My name's Al.
But you can call me Alexandria."
Which makes everyone laugh.

And we crack up again when the guy next to her,
who must be at least six foot four,
says, "My name's Richard.
And I don't care *what* you call me,
as long as you *don't* call me

Big Dick."

As the Laughing Dies Down

It dawns on me
that it's *my* turn to introduce myself.
And that everyone in the room is staring at me,
waiting for me to say something clever.

My stomach does a somersault,
but then I find myself turning to Richard,
asking, "So just to clarify, then.
Is it, like, okay if we call you . . . *Little* Dick?"

And everyone cracks up—
even Richard.
A whole roomful of people
is laughing *with* me for once,
instead of *at* me.

Then, with a strange new power
surging all through me,
I say, "Oh, and my name's Robin.
But you can call me . . . Robin."
Which cracks everyone up again.

And I'm just sitting here,
feeling how amazing this feels,
when the door to the studio swings open
and a woman rushes in—

a woman so incredibly hot
that my heart starts bouncing
off the walls of my chest
like a puck in an air hockey game.

Felix Hurries Over to Greet Her

"Ah! Chelsea!" he says,
helping her off with her coat.
"Sorry I'm late, Felix."
"On the contrary, my dear.
Your timing is exquisite."

And that's not the only thing that's exquisite.
Now that Chelsea's coat is off,
I can see that she's wearing
a tight-fitting pale pink sweater
and jeans that cling to her like shrink-wrap.

Felix leads her over to a raised wooden platform
directly in front of my easel,
and she steps up onto it.
There's nothing on the platform but an old couch,
a moth-eaten rug, and a space heater.

She sits down on the couch,
and starts to remove her boots.
"Chelsea will be our model today," Felix says,
"And we're lucky to have her—
she's one of the very best."

Our model . . . ?
Now she pulls off her socks,
revealing feet that are as flawless as the rest of her.
Oh, I get it.
We're gonna draw Chelsea's feet . . .

But then—she slips out of her jeans

and pulls her sweater off over her head
and she isn't wearing any underwear
and it all happens so fast that I feel like
I've been struck by a bolt of lightning

right between the legs.

Yikes!

My first impulse
is to avert my eyes.
My second
is to stare.

But after following
my first impulse for a while,
I decide it would be much more interesting
to follow my second one.

So I stop studying my feet,
and start studying Chelsea—
in all of her buck-naked glory . . .

I'm trying to pay attention
to what Felix is saying about discovering
the beauty of the human form.
I really am.

But I'm just a wee bit
distracted right now—
discovering the beauty
of *Chelsea's* human form!

Felix Gives Each of Us a Stick of Charcoal

Then he asks Chelsea to begin
with five two-minute poses.
She swivels her hips,
reaches toward me with both arms,
then looks off sharply to the left.

Felix tells us to dive right in.
"Try to create the illusion," he says,
"of movement and three-dimensionality."

But it's Chelsea's third dimension
that's *getting* to me,
that's making it impossible for me
to even *think* about drawing right now.

So when the two-minute timer beeps,
my paper's still as blank as the face of a liar.

Chelsea takes a new pose,
raising her arms over her head,
turning to gaze at a spot just past my right ear.

Felix wanders from easel to easel.
"Try to capture that complex mix
of skin, muscle, bone, and spirit . . ."

But I'm having a real hard time
just getting past skin—

the creamy, smooth, shimmery skin
that's covering all three
of Chelsea's delicious dimensions.

I Am One Sick Dude

I mean, this is supposed to be about art.
This is *not* supposed to be
about sex.

This is supposed to be
about discovering the beauty
of the human form.

Not about me sitting here
fantasizing sneaking off into the supply closet
with the model.

This is supposed to be about tracing
the contours of her body with my charcoal,
not with my fingers.

Besides.
I've got a girlfriend.
An unbelievably wonderful girlfriend.

I shouldn't be having these kinds of thoughts
about another woman.
That's *not* what this is supposed to be about.

When the Two-Minute Timer Beeps Again

Chelsea weaves her hands
into the tumble of blonde waves
clipped up at the nape of her neck,
and juts a perfectly curved hip
in my direction.

Suddenly, Felix is standing right next to me.
"This line here . . ." he says,
sketching a vertical mark
onto my embarrassingly blank paper,
"this line dividing the breasts is the sternum."

Then he crosses that first mark
with a horizontal one.
"And this line here is the clavicle," he says.
"Now, see how Chelsea's left breast
looks higher than her right one from this angle?"

"Sure . . ." I say, even though I *don't*.
Because I'm way too busy
staring at Chelsea's breasts
to bother noticing if one of them
looks higher than the other.

Felix glances over at me.
"Do you ever lie about anything, Robin?"
"I . . . uh . . . I . . ." I stammer.
"Is that a trick question?"
Felix chuckles.

Then he says, "When you notice one breast

is higher than the other—
lie, and make it even higher.
Human beings tend to be conservative,
so if you lie, you'll probably be closer to the truth."

"I see what you mean," I say.
And what's weird is, I sort of *do*.
"Now, just relax and get started, Robin.
Coax the images onto the page.
And, what*ever* you do—

don't think."

Don't Think?

Okay, then.
I won't think . . .
I won't think . . .
I won't think . . .

I'll just press my charcoal to the page, like this,
and begin by drawing Chelsea's . . .
by drawing Chelsea's . . . arm!
Yeah. I'll start with her arm.

And I won't think about the fact
that she's totally naked.
Totally naked
and standing just a few feet away from me.

I won't think about how good she smells.
Or about how full her lips are.
Or about how it would feel
to run my hands all over her naked body.

And I won't think about Sophie.
Or about how it would feel to run my hands
all over *her* naked body.
Or about what *she'd* look like with no clothes on.

Or about what she'll *say*
when she sees the picture
that I'm drawing of Chelsea
right *now*!

Is My Nose Growing?

Sophie's
eyebrows do a high jump.
"Whoa!" she says. "You told me
she was naked, but I didn't know she was
this naked!" I laugh nervously. "Neither did
I," I say. "I was pretty shocked when she took
off all her clothes." Sophie studies the drawing.
Then asks to see the next one. And then the next.
"These are good, Robin. *Really* good. And what's so
neat is that you got better and better with each drawing you did." There are lots of sketches to show Sophie
because after the two-minute poses, Felix had Chelsea do a bunch of longer
ones. "So, how did it feel to draw a nude model?" Sophie asks. "Oh, you know,"
I say. "It felt . . . artistic. Like it wasn't sexual or anything." Suddenly, I hear Felix's voice in my
head: "Do you ever lie about
anything, Robin?" And that's when
my cheeks start sizzling. Sophie
folds her arms across her chest;
then she grins at me
and says, "You are
soooooooooo busted."

I Don't Think I'll Ever Get Tired of This:

Of letting
my fingers

swirl across the silky skin
on Sophie's hands

while she swirls hers
across mine,

lacing
and unlacing,

in this kind of floaty,
fingertip dance . . .

both of us practically
in a trance.

At School on Wednesday Morning

I'm just
cruising along,
thinking about Sophie

and about how much I love her
and about how awesome it is
that *she* loves *me* . . .

thinking about my drawing class
and about how great Chelsea's body is
and about how I can hardly wait to draw it again . . .

just cruising along,
thinking that my life might actually
be looking up . . .

when I walk into the boys' bathroom
and find all these real sick things
scrawled across every flat surface—

things about Sophie
and what she supposedly likes to do to me,
and to *all* the boys at school.

Seeing *my* name written
on the bathroom wall
is nothing new.

But seeing *Sophie's* name up there
makes me feel like there's a writhing mass of eels
churning in my stomach.

On My Way to Lunch

I catch sight of her
heading into the girls' bathroom,
so I walk over to the water fountain to wait for her.

But a couple of seconds later,
I see Rachel and Grace rushing *out* of the bathroom,
their faces so white they could pass for mimes.

I duck out of sight around the corner
before they notice me,
but I can still hear everything:

"God," Rachel says.
"Who could have *written* all that stuff?"
"How the heck am *I* supposed to know?" Grace says.

"Did you see the look on Fee's face
when she saw it?" Rachel says.
"I wanted to say something to her, but . . ."

"I wanted to say something to her, too," Grace says.
"Like: 'What did you expect, girl?
Date a loser, turn *into* a loser.'"

"Oh, come on," Rachel says. "Fee's not a loser.
It's just that . . . just that her brain's been . . .
it's been temporarily taken over by . . . by aliens!"

"Take. Me. To. Your. Loser," Grace says,
in a space-creature-monotone voice.
And both of them crack up.

When Sophie Finally Comes Out of the Bathroom

Her eyes are all puffy.

I tell her that I heard Rachel and Grace talking—
that I'm sure they weren't the ones who did it.

But it doesn't seem to do much
to improve her mood.

And when I ask her if maybe she'd like
to skip the cafeteria today,

maybe try eating outside in the bleachers instead,
where we can have some privacy,

she doesn't tell me not to be ridiculous.
She doesn't shout, "Outlaws rule!"

She just nods,
without saying anything.

And my heart grinds to a halt.

Lunch in the Bleachers Is Okay, I Guess

Cold enough to freeze a person's butt off.
But okay.

Even though we're both feeling darker
than the sky scowling overhead.

Still, it's a relief to be together
when no one else is around.

We joke a little.
Eat a little.
Even kiss a little.

But *these* kisses are different.
They're sad, somehow.
Like echoes of kisses.

We hold hands a little.
And talk a little.

But it's like we're having
one conversation with our mouths

and an entirely *different* conversation
with our eyes.

As Soon as School Gets Out

Sophie runs up to me at the goalpost.
And when we kiss,
her lips on mine are like CPR—
breathing the life right back into me . . .

When we finally pull apart,
Sophie says, "We can't let them beat us, Robin.
They'll get tired of it, tired of *us*.
And then they'll stop."

"What makes you so sure?" I ask.
But before she even has a chance to answer,
I say, "Wait. Let me guess—
sometimes you just *know* things, right?"

Sophie grins at me and punches my arm.
"Exactly," she says.
"Well," I say, "You're not the *only* one
who knows things sometimes."

"Oh yeah?" she says. "What do *you* know?"
"I know what I like . . ." I say,
pulling her to me
for another kiss.

Then We Head Straight Over to *My* House

Because both my parents
will still be at work.

As soon as we get inside the front door,
we're all over each other.

This is what I've been waiting for the whole day.
This is what kept me going.

This is why I could stand all that sick stuff
that happened at school—

because I knew
that *this* was coming.

And now that it's finally here,
everything else disappears.

There's nothing but
Sophie's lips locked to mine . . .

Sophie's arms around my waist . . .
Sophie's hips pressing . . .

Nothing but
Sophie . . . Sophie . . . Sophie . . .

Then All of a Sudden

We hear the faint sound of my parents
singing along with Mick Jagger to "Satisfaction,"
blaring on the car radio.

Oh, no!
They're home early from Happy Time,
the preschool that they run.

Which means Sophie and I
have to put an untimely end
to our *own* happy time.

We dash into the living room, switch on the TV,
and fling ourselves down
onto opposite ends of the couch,

trying to look all innocent and un-mussed-up
and like our hearts aren't thumping
faster than jackhammers.

And a second later,
when Mom and Dad walk into the room,
Sophie and I appear to be riveted

to an episode of *Clifford the Big Red Dog*.

Here's What I'd Like to Know

How come whenever
I'm watching TV with Sophie,
and my parents
happen to walk into the room,

that's always the exact moment
when a commercial for Viagra comes on,
and some real deep-voiced announcer
says something like:

"And remember—
contact your doctor
if your erection lasts longer
than four hours"?

As I Head Up the Ramp to the Carpenter Center

To the second meeting of the drawing class,
I notice this real sexy girl strutting toward me,
the type of girl you always see
grinding around on MTV.

She's wearing a little tiger-striped jacket,
a skirt no wider than a ribbon,
and these thigh-high spike-heeled boots
that make her look tall enough to play in the WNBA.

When she's just a few yards away from me,
she flashes a smile in my direction
and says, "Nice hat."

I glance over my shoulder
to see who she's talking to.
But nobody's there.

Then, a second later,
when we're almost next to each other,
she flashes another smile, right *at* me,
and says, "And your beard's not bad either, babe."

Babe? Did she just call me *babe*?
I turn and watch her wiggle away into the night.
Then I float the rest of the way to class,
making a mental note to always wear my hat

and *never* shave again.

But Then I Get to Thinking . . .

Was it wrong
for me to have gotten
such a kick out of it just now,
when that girl called me babe?

Wouldn't *any* guy love being flirted with
by a girl who looks like that,
even if that guy already happened to have
an amazing girlfriend?

And speaking of girlfriends,
is it like a totally sick thing
that I'm wishing Sophie could have been here
to see that girl flirt with me just now?

But, I mean,
wouldn't it have made her feel good to find out
that she isn't the only girl in the world
who thinks I'm sexy?

And speaking of sexy,
is it way messed up that I'm so excited
about seeing Chelsea's naked body again
a few minutes from now?

Am I just
a normal red-blooded American guy?
Or a deluded and disgusting
pervy dawg?

When I Walk into Studio B

Felix tips an imaginary hat to me,
and everybody else calls out "Hey!" or "Yo!"
or gives me a little wave.
Except for Tessa, who flashes me the peace sign
and says, "'Sup, Wild Thing?"

A second later,
when I sit down in front of my easel,
I get that same feeling you get
when you walk outside on the first real warm day
after a winter that seemed like it would never end.

And I can't help thinking how glad I am
that Felix hasn't told anyone I'm still in high school.
Because for the first time in my life,
I actually feel like I fit in
with a whole group of people.

And I'm in no hurry for that feeling to go away.

Tessa and I Are Sharpening Our Pencils
Before Class

"Okay," she says. "Pop quiz: Which girl group
had the first number one hit?"
I'm debating between the Chiffons and the Shirelles,
when this big fat middle-aged woman
waddles in through the door of the studio.

I figure she's probably just
the cleaning lady or something.
But Felix hurries over to help her off with her coat.
Then he tells the class that her name is Gina.
And that she'll be modeling for us tonight.

Gina's gonna be our model?
But what happened to Chelsea?
To incredibly beautiful Chelsea
who I've been dreaming about seeing
all day?

When Felix says
Gina's very different from Chelsea,
I think to myself, *Duh* . . .
But when he says
she's every bit as amazing as Chelsea,

I think, *Geez. This guy needs glasses!*

Gina Hoists Herself Up onto the Platform

And slips out of her loose-fitting dress.

Eeewww . . . This is *not* the kind of person
you want to see without her underwear on:
hippopotamus thighs, breasts like saggy blimps,
butt cheeks big as planets . . .

Felix asks Gina to take her first pose.
"It's not about trying
to trace Gina's edges," he tells us,
"it's about imagining you're wrapping her in ribbon."

The idea of wrapping Gina in *anything*
grosses me out.
Though when I start sketching her,
something weird happens.

I realize that with all of her bulges and bumps
and extra rolls of fat,
she's even more fun to draw
than Chelsea.

There's something about all her mounds of roundness
that reminds me of a bunch of ripe grapes,
or of one of those real curvy women
in all those paintings by Rubens.

In fact, the more I look at Gina,
the more I can see
that she *is* every bit as amazing as Chelsea—
just like Felix said.

During Gina's Break

Tessa gives Honk and me
another one of her pop quizzes:

"Who said,
'The Beatles saved the world from boredom'?"
I slam my hand down on an imaginary buzzer.
"I believe that would be George Harrison."

But Honk doesn't even *pretend* to have a clue.
"Didn't Kanye West say that?" he asks,
before taking off with Eve
to try to find a Coke machine.

Then I say, "Okay, Tessa. Which Beatle
had the most successful solo career
for the first five years after the group broke up?"

She doesn't even have to think about it.
"That's easy," she says.
"It was Ringo."

No one knows that!
I can't believe she got it right.
I gotta give her props.

"Until *you* came along," I say,
"I'd never met another teenager
who knows as much about old rock and roll as I do."

She grins at me and says, "You still haven't—
I don't know *as much* about

old rock and roll as you do,
I know *more* about it than you do."

"Oh, yeah?" I say,
racking my brain for a way to stump her.
"Then what grade were Simon and Garfunkel in
when they first met?"

"Sixth," she says, without missing a beat.
Dang, she's good.

Class Is Over

I'm rolling up my sketches,
when I overhear Honk asking Eve and Tessa
if they want to go get something to eat.

Honk suggests Café Paradiso,
but he gets outvoted by the other two,
who say they like Finale better.

As I listen to the three of them hatching their plan,
that old familiar left-out feeling
drifts down over me like a sad song.

Then, out of the blue,
Eve turns to me and says,
"You coming with us, Robin?"

And she says this
like it's no big deal.
Like of *course* I'm included.

"You better, man," Honk says.
"Or these two bodacious babes might try
to take unfair advantage of me."

I'm Just About to Leap on Their Offer

When it suddenly hits me—
Mom's probably already waiting for me.
And I bet she's parked *right out front*!

If I walk out there with these guys
and they see her waving at me or something,
they might figure out how young I am.

What should I do?
There's no time to sneak off and call her on my cell.
Besides. What would I say to her?
"Quick, Mom! Hide?"

So I say, "Thanks, guys. I wish I could.
But I've gotta be somewhere."
Then I hightail it out of there.

And a second later, I'm racing down the stairs,
my feet in a Road-Runnery blur,
when this real bizarre feeling comes over me—
like I'm the male equivalent of Cinderella,

and if I don't make it to Mom's Volvo
before the clock strikes twelve,
it's gonna turn back into a pumpkin.

And *I'm*
gonna turn back
into Murphy.

Though I Guess It Doesn't Really Matter

Because I always *do* turn back into Murphy.
Every time I walk through the door
of Cambridge High.

I turn back into Murphy,
and *Sophie* turns into that strange girl,
the one who's actually going *out* with Murphy,

the girl who used to be normal,
who used to be popular,
who used to have two best friends,

two best friends
who turned into two *ex*–best friends
the second they found out Sophie was dating *me*,

two ex–best friends
who won't even talk to her anymore,
who just look away when they see her,

or put their heads together
and whisper about
that strange girl,

the one
who's actually going out
with Murphy.

Dylan Just Stole My Hat Again

Only *this* time,
he didn't throw it out the window.
This time he shoved it down onto his *own* head
and started dancing around.

"Look at me. Look at me," he sang.
"I'm Murphy. I'm fugly."
And all the people in the hall cracked up,
like he'd just said the most hilarious thing ever.

I tried to grab it back,
but he kept ducking out of my reach.
Then, when the bell rang,
he slam-dunked it into the trash can and took off.

I rushed over to fish it out,
but it was too late—
the brim already had a glob
of unidentifiable greenish-brown slime on it . . .

And now I'm just standing here
trying to wipe it off,
feeling about as powerless
as a dead battery.

It's 4:00 p.m.

And Sophie and I
are back at Adrenaline Zone,
getting ready to start cruisin' the U.S.A.

We're sitting next to each other,
me—revving the motor
of a virtual pimped-out Mustang,

she—
gripping the wheel
of a glittery pink Thunderbird.

But something tells me
that when that starting flag goes down,
neither one of us will be trying to win the race.

We'll just be ramming as many of those
poor, defenseless, cud-chewing cows as we can,
trying to turn them into steaks.

Okay.
Maybe it *is* sick.
But it's a whole lot cheaper than therapy.

On the Way Over to My Third Class at Harvard

I tell Mom I think I'd feel more inspired
if I got a little exercise before my art classes.
"So from now on, why don't you just drop me off
at this corner and I'll walk from here?"

She looks at me a little funny, but she pulls over.
She seems like she wants to say something to me,
though all she does is brush the hair off my forehead.
Which sort of makes my skin crawl, but I let her.

Then I tell her I'll probably be going out
for dessert after class with some of the other students
(maybe they won't even ask me this time,
but I've got to be ready in case they *do*).

"Well, okay . . ." she says. "Though it *is* a school night.
And you know how you get
when you don't have enough sleep and . . ."
Blah dee blah blah blah.

Just what I need—to be treated like a toddler
by my overprotective mommy.
"Don't come till I *call* you," I say,
leaping out of the car.

And as I dash down the sidewalk,
she shouts after me, "Be safe!"
Like she thinks if she didn't say that,
I'd be—what?

*Un*safe?

Before Class

Honk and I start messing around with Dr. Bones,
the life-size human skeleton
that's hanging from a metal stand
in the corner of the room.

Honk slips a tube of Super Glue out of his pocket,
glances around to make sure Felix hasn't arrived,
then glues a thin strip
of stiff red carpet onto its skull.
"Whoa. Dude . . ." I say. "Instant Mohawk."

I move Dr. Bones's jaw so it looks like he's talking.
"Yo! Tessa! Eve!" I make him shout,
lifting his arm to point at his head.
"How do you like my new 'do?"

The girls look over at us and grin,
then join us in the corner.
"No offense, Dr. Bones," Eve says,
"but you are having a seriously bad hair day."
I move Dr. B's hand to his mouth like he's horrified.

"Sticks and stones may break my bones,"
I make him say.
"But who cares? I'm already dead."
And when the three of them bust out laughing,

I feel like the funniest guy on Earth.

Geez

Now I've seen everything.

In fact, I've seen way more
than I actually *wanted* to see.

Because tonight's model isn't Chelsea.
Tonight's model isn't Gina.

Tonight's model is Wade:
one totally nude

dude!

This Is So . . .

. . . Awkward.
To just be sitting here
staring at a naked man like this.

Because, let's face it.
Guys don't usually sit around staring
at guys who aren't wearing any clothes.

Like, in the men's room,
when you're standing there
peeing next to someone—

it's not exactly socially acceptable
to check out what that other guy
is holding in his hand.

And it is even *less* socially acceptable
to keep your eyes anywhere but straight ahead
when you're taking a communal shower after P.E.

So,
when it comes right down to it,
I haven't actually *seen* a lot of penises.

And sitting here
staring at this completely nude male model
is kind of weirding me out.

Because . . . well . . .
let's just say I hope Wade's wang
is *way* above average.

What It's Not About

"It's not about surfaces . . ." Felix says
as he wanders from easel to easel.
"It's about what's *below* the surface."
So I try to see below Wade's surface,
while avoiding the area below Wade's waist.

"It's not about making pictures . . ." Felix says
as he continues through the room.
"It's about *seeing*.
It's not about knowing . . .
It's about being obedient to the shape that you see."

Geez. I'd *be* obedient to it—if I could *locate* it.
But Wade's pretty shapeless.
I mean, compared to Chelsea and Gina.
"Meander around till you find it," Felix says.
"Just follow the bouncing ball."

Follow the bouncing ball?
What the heck does he mean by *that*?
I glance over at Eve and catch her eye.
But she just shrugs and gives me a look
like, "Don't ask *me*."

When Class Is Over

Honk says, "Who wants to go get something to eat?"

I'm trying to work up the courage to say, "Me,"
when Eve takes hold of my left hand,
Tessa takes hold of my right one,
and Eve says, "*We* do."
Like it's a done deal.

"Mind if we kidnap you?" Tessa asks.
"It's not about being kidnapped . . ." I say,
doing my best Felix impression.
"It's about being *obedient* to your kidnappers."
Which cracks them both up.

"Okay, then, people," Honk says,
turning to head toward the door,
then pausing to waggle his butt at us.
"Just follow my bouncing balls."
Which causes a loud chorus of eeewwws.

"It's not about being disgusting . . ." Tessa says,
swatting Honk with her rolled-up sketches.
"It's about being *truly* disgusting."
And as we head out the door, Richard calls after us,
"Hey! Don't meander off without *me*!"

Then, the five of us pile into the elevator,
and there's a few seconds
when no one says anything.
Finally, Eve blurts out,
"Can you believe how *gigantic* that guy was?"

And when everyone bursts out laughing,
I can't help noticing
that Honk and Richard
look almost as relieved
as *I* am.

At Café Paradiso

We squeeze into a tiny booth and order our desserts.
Then Tessa tosses out another one of her pop quizzes:
"Okay," she says. "What famous rock and roller said,
'I don't know anything about music.
In *my* line of business, you don't have to'?"

"Elvis," I say instantly. "Next question?"
Tessa groans and tries to strangle me,
but Richard restrains her.
"Use your words, Tessa, use your words . . ."
She growls at him, then fires off another one:

"Who said, 'Instead of getting married again,
I'm just going to find a woman I don't like
and give her a house'?"
"Beats me," Honk says. "Me too," Richard says.
"I believe that would be Rod Stewart," I say,
ducking behind Eve for protection.

Tessa slaps her forehead.
"Damn! You are positively unstumpable!"
"Bro," Honk says, "if we ever play Trivial Pursuit,
I want you on *my* team."
"Seriously," Eve says.

And as I look around the table at everyone,
I think to myself,
"So this is how it feels
to hang with a whole table full of people
who don't even know

what a Murphy *is*."

Unlike, Say, All the People at Cambridge High

Who know full *well* what a Murphy is.
And make it a point not to let me forget it.

So school sucked today.
For all the usual reasons:

Rachel and Grace ignored Sophie.
Again.

Dylan swiped my hat.
Again.

And all day long,
wherever Sophie and I went,

random people
committed random acts

of unkindness.

Bowling with a Vengeance

Here's the way
Sophie and I play:

we take aim,
think of a name,

imagine those pins
are teeth or shins,

pull back our arm
for maximum harm,

then let the ball fly—
an eye for an eye.

You get the gist?
That ball's a fist.

We bowl
with one goal:

hurl that sucker
down the lane

and inflict
pain.

The Door to Studio B Swings Open

And Richard enters,
talking to a real tall girl
who's wearing this little tiger-striped jacket
and these thigh-high spike-heeled boots and—

Whoa!
It's that girl who flirted with me!
That sexy refugee from MTV.
The one who called me "babe."

As she struts toward me,
sizzling like a lit fuse,
my mind struggles to invent an explanation
for what she could possibly be doing here:

She must be a friend of Richard's.
No—she must be his *sister*; they're both so tall.
No—she's probably a transfer student,
joining the class a week late.

When she sees me,
a smile oozes onto her face like spilled honey.
And when she blinks at me, in sultry slow motion,
it's like an invitation to a *very* private party.

Then, in a voice as deep as a French kiss,
she says, "Hello again."
And I almost fall over—
she *remembers* me?

So, with what I hope will pass

as a rakish grin,
I say, "Are you stalking me?"
She laughs and says, "Absolutely, babe."

Wow!
She did it again—
she called me "babe"!
She must think I'm really *hot* . . .

And Then Without Any Warning

Before I even have a chance
to grasp what's happening,

before I even have a chance
to gasp,

she steps up onto the platform,
right in front of me,

unzips
her thigh-high boots,

and five seconds later—
she's stark raving naked!

Honk's Elbow Snaps Me Out of My Daze

"You *know* her?" he whispers,
with this real "omigod" sort of gleam in his eyes.
"When you gonna introduce *me* to her?"

But Felix beats me to it.
"People," he says, "allow me to present Berry.
Isn't she incredible?"

Yeah, I think to myself.
Berry incredible.
And so is this situation . . .

Felix gazes at her thoughtfully, then says,
"Would you please take a horizontal pose
and hold it for five minutes?"

And that's when Berry
blinks at *Felix* in sultry slow motion,
like she's inviting *him* to a very private party,

and says, "Sure thing . . . babe."

I Loiter After Class

And time it so that I end up in the elevator
with Honk, Tessa, Eve, and Richard,

hoping maybe they'll get the bright idea
to invite me out to eat with them again.

As soon as the doors slide shut,
they start debating where to dine—

the girls arguing for Café Algiers,
the guys for the Greenhouse.

No one even thinks of asking me if *I* want to come.
I guess four's company, five's a crowd.

So I just stand here staring at my sneakers,
with my heart falling faster than the elevator.

But then Eve slips her arm through mine
and says, "Which one do *you* want to go to, Robin?"

"Yeah, bro," Honk says,
tossing his arm over my shoulder.

"We're counting on you to settle the tie."

At Café Algiers

Tessa tears into her lamb kebab.
"Mmm . . ." she says.
"I'd almost forgotten how good real food tastes."

"Me, too," Honk says, scarfing down his falafel.
"I'm so fed up with that inedible crap
they serve in the freshman dining hall."

"Seriously," Richard says.
"What was that disgusting concoction
they tried to palm off on us tonight?"

"The sign said 'beef fajita fettuccini,'" Eve says.
"Whatsa matter you, señorita?" I say.
"You got something against Mexican Italians?"

Which cracks everyone up,
and helps to distract them from wondering
why they've never seen *me* in the dining hall.

And a minute later, when they all start talking
about what classes they're taking,
I excuse myself nonchalantly

and head off to the bathroom.

I Tell Sophie

That I don't exactly know
if things at school have been much worse lately,
or if it only *seems* that way in comparison
to when I'm hanging with the people at Harvard.

Because when I'm with *them*,
it's like I'm living in an alternate universe—
a universe where Murphy is just
my last name.

I tell Sophie that when I'm at Harvard
I feel like a completely different person,
because I'm not the *butt* of the jokes;
I'm the one *telling* them.

And Sophie tells *me*
how happy she is for me.
How I'm just getting
what I've deserved all along.

So I *don't* tell her that the best part of all
is that when I'm at Harvard,
I get to take a little break
from feeling like a total scumbag

for wrecking her life.

Don't Get Me Wrong

I mean, Sophie never tries
to make me feel guilty or anything.
In fact, she tries real hard
not to make me feel guilty.

But when we're at school
and I see how everyone's treating her,
it pretty much makes me want to throw myself
under the wheels of a Hummer.

Like today, in the cafeteria,
when we walked by Rachel and Grace's table.
Sophie said hey, but they just acted as if
she wasn't even a blip on their radar screen.

Which really got to me.
Because even though Sophie tried to pretend
like she couldn't care less,
I saw the lights in her eyes flicker

and go out.

T.G.I.F.

I'm heading to English class,
in a kind of near-dream state,
thinking about how there's only
ninety-seven minutes left till the final bell rings,

thinking that if Sophie and I can just manage
to survive till the end of this endless week,
we'll finally be able to escape from this Alcatraz
and spend some time *alone* together.

Because on Saturday
my parents are heading up to Vermont
to this weird preschool convention
that they go to every February.

Which means Sophie and I will have
the house to ourselves all day long!

So I'm practically floating down the corridor,
thinking about how we're gonna be
alone in my kitchen, alone in my living room,
alone in my bedroom, alone in my bed . . .

when I happen to turn the corner
just in time to see Grace trip over
her own Converse high-tops and go flying.
Just in time to see her crash to the floor.

Just in time to hear everyone within earshot
start snickering when Dylan shouts out,
"Whoa . . . Grace . . .
You are *such* a Stein."

Such a *What?!*

I stagger back,
feeling like a rifle blast
has just torn my chest to shreds.

He couldn't have said
what I think he said,
could he?

But the answer slaps me hard
across the face:
He *said* it, all right.

And he didn't even see me
when I came around the corner.
So he couldn't have only been saying it
to *get* to me.

He was just saying it.
Like it was the most natural thing
in the world to say.

Like it was something
people say all the time.
Which means—

Oh, God!
They probably *do* say it
all the time!

NO . . .

NO . . .

NO . . .

NO . . .

NO . . .

NO . . .

NO . . .

NO!!!

I've Got to Get Away from Here

Got to be alone . . .
but where?

I stumble down the hall,
find the bathroom door,

shove it open quick,
rush into a stall,

lock the door behind me,
lean against the wall,

and let the tears
fall.

I'm Waiting for Sophie After School

Right here by the goalpost, like I always do.

But now that I've caught sight of her,
hurrying across the field to me
like a dream come true,
with such a big smile on her face
that I can even make it out from here,

now that I've seen
how carefree she looks,
how unsuspecting,
how totally clueless she is
about what I'm getting ready to do—

I suddenly realize
that there's just no *way*
that I'll be able
to do it.

And Before I Even Know What's Happening

I'm running—
running as far away
and as fast away
from Sophie as I can get.

Sprinting past the bleachers,
cutting through the bushes,
racing down the sidewalk,
not looking back.

I'm running
from having to face her,
running from having to tell her,
running from having to say it out loud:

we're going to have to break up.

But Just Thinking About Having to Do That

Makes me feel like a nuclear bomb
is whizzing straight toward me.

We have to break up, though.
We *have* to.

Because people have started treating Sophie
like they've always treated me.

And I wouldn't wish that
on my worst enemy.

Well, actually, maybe I *would* wish that
on my worst enemy.

But I sure wouldn't wish it
on Sophie.

When I Get Home

Mom takes one look at me,
then hurries over
and gives me a quick, fierce hug.

She tries to brush the hair off my forehead,
but I duck out of reach.
"Want me to make you some hot cocoa?" she says.

"No, thanks," I say, running up the stairs.
"And if Sophie comes to see me or calls,
tell her I'm not home, okay?"

"Well . . .
if that's what you
really *want* me to do . . ."

"Just *do* it!" I scream,
suddenly gripped by an overwhelming urge
to put my fist right through the wall.

Then I rage into my bedroom,
slam the door behind me,
fling myself onto the bed,

and smash my pillow down over my face.

A Few Minutes Later, the Doorbell Rings

I hear the sound
of the front door opening.

I hear the murmur of Sophie's voice
mingled with Mom's.

I hear the sound
of the door closing.

I go to the window
and watch Sophie walking away.

Even her *back*
looks sad . . .

I Fling Myself Back onto My Bed

And just then, my cell phone rings,
jolting me like a zap from a Taser.
It's got to be Sophie!

(No one else even has the number
except for my parents.)

I rush over to my backpack
and start digging for it,
like I'm this half-starved dog
and there's a nice meaty bone buried in there.

But when I finally find it,
I don't answer it.

I just stand here staring at it,
beeping away in the palm of my hand.
And then—

I switch it off.

At Dinnertime

My parents
don't even ask me
if I want to come down.

They just show up at my bedroom door
with a steaming bowl
of chicken noodle soup
on a tray.

Man . . .
my favorite food
from when I was little . . .
I almost lose it.

"Thanks," I manage to croak.
"No problem," Dad says,
giving me a thumbs-up.

Then he cocks his head to the side,
the way he always does
when he's worried about me,

like I'm this message
written in a secret code
that he's trying real hard
to crack.

Mom reaches
to brush the hair off my forehead,
and this time,
I let her.

"You want to talk about it?" she says.
I shake my head no,
trying hard not to choke

on the enormous lump in my throat.

I Have *Got* to Get My Mind Off Sophie

I guess I'll try doing my math homework . . .

Problem:

If
a guy

wants to
avoid talking

to his girlfriend,
so he switches off

his cell phone at 4:30
p.m., but then his girlfriend

starts calling him on the land
line every ten minutes, only his

parents don't want to have to lie
and tell her he isn't home, so they

let the answering machine pick up
all the calls, but the answering machine

refuses to answer each call till the
phone's rung at least 100 times, how many

times will the phone have to ring before
the guy TOTALLY LOSES IT????????

Around Ten O'Clock

My parents slip back into my room
and sit down on the edge of my bed.
A second later, the phone starts ringing,
for like the ninety-millionth time.

The three of us just sit here,
listening to it ring and ring and ring . . .
till the answering machine
finally gets around to picking it up.

Then Dad clears his throat and says,
"Your mother and I were thinking
of skipping the convention tomorrow."
"No!" I almost shout. "I'll be fine here by myself."

"Are you sure?" Mom says.
"I'm positive," I say.
"You guys don't have to worry."
"But we *like* to worry," Dad says with a grin.

"Yeah," Mom says. "We're great at worrying.
We're a couple of worrying *geniuses*."
"I've noticed that about you," I say.
And they both crack up at this,

like it was way funnier than it actually was.

Saturday Morning

I don't remember
getting out of bed
or coming down the stairs.

But I must have.

Because here I am,
sitting at the kitchen table
like a zombie.

I don't remember
grabbing hold of the telephone wire
or yanking it out of the wall.

But I must have.

Because here I am,
holding the cord
in my hand.

I don't remember
opening up the cabinet
or getting out the milk or the cereal.

But I must have.

Because here I am,
staring down into
a bowl of soggy Cheerios.

Saturday Afternoon

I've been lying on my bed for hours,
feeling as demolished as Van Gogh must have felt
right before he slashed his own ear off,

just lying here
staring at the portrait I drew of Sophie
that I've got tacked up on my wall,

when, for some reason,
I start thinking about
Honk and Eve and Tessa and Richard,

thinking about how the four of them
are the closest thing I've ever had to actual friends,
maybe the closest thing I ever *will* have.

And about how I wish I had their phone numbers
so I could call one of them up right now and
tell them my troubles, like friends *do* with friends . . .

But if I *did* that—
if I told them about Sophie and me,
told them about why I've got to break up with her,

I'd have to admit that I'm still just in high school.
And then I'd have to explain
about the whole Murphy thing.

Which would make me feel *twice* as demolished
as Van Gogh must have felt
right before he slashed his own ear off.

Oh, No!

The doorbell's ringing!
Sophie?
I rush over to the window
and peek through the curtain.

But it's only Mrs. Jeffries,
the cranky old ball thief who lives next to us.
I tramp down the stairs and pull open the door.
"What on Earth *took* you so long?" she says.

But she doesn't wait for me to answer.
She launches right in,
telling me that the only reason
she dragged herself all the way over here
is because my parents just called her.

She says they've been phoning me all day,
but they haven't been able to reach me,
so they asked her to knock on the door
to make sure I was all right.

She says I should be ashamed of myself
for worrying my folks like that,
and that if I was a *decent* young man,
I'd phone them back right this minute
and apologize.

So I force my lips into a smile and say,
"Thanks, Mrs. Jeffries. I'll give them a call."
Even though I'm *not* a decent young man.
In fact, I'm not a man at all.

I'm just a wuss.
A pathetic little wuss
who's too scared to face
his own soon-to-be-ex girlfriend.

Mom Sounds So Relieved

"Robin!" she cries. "It's you!"
"You recognized my voice," I say,
making a feeble attempt at humor.

I can almost feel
the feathery touch of her fingers
on my forehead.

She asks me how I am.
And I tell her I'm fine.
But both of us know I'm lying.

Then Dad gets on the line
and tells me there's a blizzard
falling in Vermont.

So they won't be able
to make it home
until the morning.

Suddenly I feel like I'm Wile E. Coyote,
and Road Runner's just flattened me
with another one of those Acme anvils.

Because what good will it do me
to have the house all to myself,
if Sophie isn't here

to be alone *with* me?

Now Mom Gets Back on the Line

"Promise me you'll leave the phone plugged in.
You can let the machine answer all the calls.
But that way, if you hear it's us,
you can still pick up."

So I say that I will,
and then I apologize for worrying them—
as per my annoying next-door neighbor's
instructions.

But as soon as I say good-bye,
Mrs. Jeffries starts ringing the bell again.
And she's *really* leaning on it
this time.

The echoing clang of it
ricochets off the walls of my skull.
Why won't old Freezerface
just leave me alone?

I do *not* feel like dealing with her right now.
But it doesn't sound like she's getting ready
to stop beating up on our bell anytime soon.
So I guess there's no way out of it . . .

I trudge back over to the door
and yank it open.
Only it's not Mrs. Jeffries—
it's *Sophie*!

My Heart Catapults Up Into My Throat

Then boomerangs
right back down
into my feet.

I never knew a person could feel
like jumping for joy
and jumping off a bridge

at the exact
same
moment.

I Don't Know What to Do

So I don't do anything.
And neither does Sophie.

She just stands there
watching me squirm,
with this almost smile on her lips,
her arms folded across her chest,
her cheeks all rosed from the cold,
her eyes shooting sparks straight into mine,

looking so outrageously beautiful
that I just about keel over.

I want to scoop her up into my arms.
I want to grab her and kiss her.
I want to zip our bodies together,
like we're two halves of the same sleeping bag.
But I just stand here,
with my arms pressed stiffly to my sides.

Because I can't do *any* of that stuff with her.
Ever again.

And I'm Gonna Have to Tell Her That

Right *now*.
But just as I'm about to open my mouth
and force the awful words out,

Sophie brushes past me,
marching straight up the stairs
and down the hall toward my bedroom.

I watch her disappear through the door,
and my heart starts flopping around in my chest
like a fish fighting for its life.

I'm gonna have to walk right up those same stairs
and tell her it's over between us.
Even if it kills me—which it definitely will.

So I force myself to spring into action,
like Spider-Man on a mission,
and sprint up the steps two at a time.

But a second later,
when I burst into my room,
Sophie doesn't even glance up.

She's sitting on my bed,
drawing something on the huge sketch pad
that I keep by my desk.

I open my mouth to speak.
But the words refuse to cooperate,
cowering in the back of my throat like scared dogs.

When Sophie Finally Looks Up at Me

Her face is a neutral mask.
She motions for me to
sit down next to her on the bed,
then continues crisscrossing the paper
with straight black lines,
separating the sheet into what look like
the empty frames of a page out of a comic book.

Then she starts filling in the first frame,
while I sit here next to her,
watching her drawing take shape,
trying to ignore the shivers
that ripple all through me
every time the smooth, warm skin
of her bare arm brushes up against mine.

Sophie's drawing a picture of a girl—
a girl who looks a lot like *her*.
The girl's standing in the middle
of a snow-covered football field,
watching a boy who's running away from her.
Sophie draws a teardrop
trickling down the girl's cheek.

Next, she adds a thought cloud
above the girl's head.
But she doesn't write any words inside of it.
She just draws this big question mark.
And then she passes the pencil
and the sketch pad
back to me.

So I Start Working on the Second Frame

I draw a close-up of the boy.
(Guess who *he* looks like.)

I draw him
with this expression on his face

like maybe someone just told him
he flunked out of school.

Or that his house
just burned down to the ground.

Or that he's got to tell his girlfriend
he's breaking up with her.

Even though
just *thinking* about doing that

makes him feel like
he's having open-heart surgery—

with*out* an anesthetic.

When I Finish the Boy's Face

I draw a thought cloud above his head.
And inside of it, I write:
I CAN'T TELL HER ...
I JUST CAN'T TELL HER ...

Then I pass the sketchbook back to Sophie,
and she draws the girl walking down the street alone,
a trail of jagged question marks
following after her like a gang of evil spirits.

And then I draw the boy,
rushing up the stairs past his mother.
And Sophie draws the girl,
knocking on the boy's front door.

And I draw the boy,
standing at the window,
watching the girl walk away—
a small figure hunched against an icicled world.

Then Sophie fills in the next frame.
And I fill in the next.
And we keep on going like this,
passing our story back and forth . . .

But I still
can't bring myself to tell her
what I've been avoiding telling her
all along.

Finally

Sophie draws a picture of the boy and the girl
sitting together on a bed.

The girl's drawing a picture
in a sketchbook.

Then Sophie passes the story
back to me,

letting her fingers touch mine
as she hands me the pencil,

sending rivers of wanting
all through me,

rivers so deep
that I ache.

But I'm Gonna Have to Learn to Live
with That Ache

So I grit my teeth
and make myself draw a picture
of myself telling Sophie
the terrible thing I heard Dylan say yesterday:

YOU ARE SUCH A STEIN.
My hand shakes when I write these words
into the speech cloud above my head.
But I make myself keep going:

AND WHEN I HEARD DYLAN *SAY* THAT,
I REALIZED I WAS GONNA HAVE TO
BREAK UP WITH—
But Sophie plucks the pencil from my hand.

She looks at me and I look at her,
and neither one of us even blinks.
Then, at the exact same moment,
we say, "I love you."

And both of us start laughing.
But sort of crying, too.
Then, at the exact same moment,
we lean in for a kiss.

And it's one of those
waves breaking,
cymbals crashing,
thunder and lightning kinds of kisses.

When We Stop to Catch Our Breath

Sophie tells me
she knows what Dylan's been saying.
She says lots of people at school have been saying it.
For weeks now.

And when she tells me this,
my heart turns to roadkill in my chest.
"I thought you knew . . ." she says.
I shake my head no.

"I'm not gonna lie," she says.
"I'm not gonna tell you it doesn't hurt.
It flips me out whenever I hear someone say it.
But we can't let those idiots break us up."

And when she wraps her arms around me,
I feel like I've been rescued.
Like I'm a passenger on the *Titanic*,
and Sophie's my lifeboat.

"Everything will work out . . ." I say. "It *will*."
"Sometimes *you* just know things, too," she says.
And we lean in
for another kiss—

the type of kiss
that if someone had been turned into a frog
and then he got a kiss like this,
it would definitely turn him back into a prince.

Or maybe even into a king.

It Feels So Good, I Don't *Ever* Want It to Stop

But, after a while,
Sophie unlocks her lips from mine.
Then, staring steamily into my eyes,
she stands up next to the bed
and slowly starts pulling off her T-shirt.

Whoa—!
I practically pass out . . .
But then I see that she's wearing
a tank top underneath it.

Dang . . . I adjust my jeans
while she grabs a marker
from the coffee can on my desk
and spreads her T-shirt out flat on the floor.

Then, in big black in-your-face letters,
she writes: I AM *SUCH* A STEIN,
and on the back she puts:
AND PROUD *OF* IT!

All of a sudden, I'm tearing off my own T-shirt,
laying it out on the floor, grabbing a marker,
and scrawling: I'M WITH STEIN.
"I *love* it!" Sophie says.

Then I reach out, pulling her in to me.
And she feels unbelievably soft
against my bare chest.
"Outlaws rule . . ." I murmur,
pressing my lips to hers.

Somehow

We end up back on my bed.
I don't even know how we got here.
Floated, probably.

We haven't taken off
any more of our clothes.
And we still haven't gone past first base.

But I sure am
starting to think about
stealing second . . .

The currents of electricity
surging between us
could light up the entire city of Cambridge.

Between kisses,
I tell Sophie that my parents
won't be coming home tonight.

"No chaperones?!" she gasps,
pretending to be horrified.
"I must inform my mother at once!"

Now we're laughing and kissing
and pressing our bodies together so hard
that it feels like we're merging—

merging
into one breathless being
with two hammering hearts . . .

And Then the Telephone Rings

I force myself to break away from Sophie
and stagger over to my bedroom door,
so I can listen when the phone machine picks up
and hear if it's my parents.

Sophie comes up close behind me,
and lets her silky hair
brush against my bare shoulders,
covering me with goose bumps

Then—"Robin?"
Mom's voice calls out through the speaker.
"Sweetie pie? Are you there? If you don't pick up,
your father and I will worry . . ."

Sophie runs her fingers lightly across my back.
Then she gives me a playful shove out the door
and says, "You better answer it.
Sweetie pie."

Grrrr . . .

Now I Switch into Hyper Gear

Because
the sooner I answer the phone,
the sooner I can get back to Sophie
to continue right where we left off.

I charge down the hall like the Energizer Bunny
and grab the phone.
"'Sup, Mom?" I say,
trying to sound all casual.

She asks me how I'm feeling,
and I tell her I'm better.
"You do sound a little more *up* . . ." she says.
"What have you been doing?"

"Oh, nothing much.
Just lying around on my bed."
Which is the God's honest truth.
In a *way*.

I Get Off the Phone as Fast as I Can

And race back down the hall
to my bedroom.
But when I get there—

Sophie's wearing
her I AM *SUCH* A STEIN shirt,
and she's slipping her jacket on over it.

She hands me my own shirt
and gives me a sheepish grin.
"I think maybe we should take a little break from . . ."

She looks over at the bed and blushes,
not even finishing her sentence.
But I get the idea.

"Want to go to the museum?" she asks.
No! I think to myself.
I don't want to go to the museum.

I want to stay right here
doing lots more of exactly what we were doing
before the phone rang!

But I just pull on my I'M WITH STEIN shirt,
slap a smile onto my face,
and say, "I'm there."

Before We Leave

I call back my parents
to tell them where I'm going.

Because if they called the house
and I didn't pick up the phone,
and then they tried my cell
but they couldn't get through
because Verizon sucks so bad,
they'd probably call Mrs. Jeffries again,
not to mention the local police and the F.B.I.

And my picture would be on
every milk carton in the country
before Sophie and I even got back to the house.

So I tell them I'm going to the museum,
but I *don't* tell them
that Sophie's going *with* me,
and that afterwards,
we're gonna be here alone together
for hours and hours
before her mother comes to pick her up.

Because not telling someone something,
when someone's not even asking,
is *not* the same thing as lying. Is it?

Besides,
I don't have to tell my parents
about every single thing
that's going on in my personal life.

In fact, I don't have to tell them
about *anything* that's going on
in my personal life.

That's why they call it
personal.

And Even if I *Did* Tell Them

They'd probably just say something like,
"We trust you implicitly."

And you know what's really annoying about that?
They actually *do* trust me.

And, frankly, that pisses me off.
Because, I mean, I'm a *teenager.*

They aren't *supposed*
to trust me.

But it's like they think I'm such a loser
that I'd never do anything wrong.

Which sort of makes me feel
like *doing* something wrong.

Just to show them.

When Worlds (Almost) Collide

Sophie and I are sketching, talking quietly,
and sneaking kisses on the wooden bench
in front of *Le Bal à Bougival*,

when I happen to glance down the corridor
and see Honk and Eve
heading right toward us!

I pull Sophie up and tell her it's time to go,
tugging her away with me
in the opposite direction.

Because if they see me,
I'll have to introduce them
to Sophie.

And I mean, what if I *do* that,
and she says something that sounds . . .
I don't know . . . sort of immature or something?

Not that Sophie's immature.
Well, I mean, she *is* immature.
But not for a fourteen-year-old.

I mean, she's just *right* for her age.
But what if she happens to mention
that she goes to Cambridge High?

Honk and Eve might figure out that *I* do, too!

We Stop Off for Pizza at Pinocchio's

Then we catch the bus back to my house
and end up going online
to try to figure out how long it'll take my parents
to drive home in the morning.

So we start looking at maps of Vermont,
and, somehow,
we end up downloading this amazing program
called Google Earth.

It's got about a zillion
photos of the world on it
that must have been taken
by satellites and airplanes and stuff.

It's hard for Sophie and me
to believe what we're seeing,
because when you type in an address,
it starts zooming in,

all the way in from, like, outer space,
right down to your own country,
and then to your own state,
and your own city,

all the way down
to your own neighborhood,
until you can actually see
the roof of your own house!

So we zoom down to Sophie's house.

And then over to my house.
And pretty soon we're zooming
all around the world—

to places like Paris and London and Rome,
dreaming about someday wandering
through the streets of those far-off places
together . . .

Then We Start Making Out

And for some reason,
just knowing that there's zero chance
of my parents walking in on us,
makes every kiss twice as intense.

It doesn't take long
for my heart to start
racing around in my chest
like it's trying to win the Indy 500.

Then—*click!*
It's like somebody aimed
the remote control at my head
and somehow put my mind on "pause."

Because,
all of a sudden,
I can't think.
I can only *feel* . . .

There's nothing but Sophie and me
and the way her arms feel wrapping around me,
the way our tongues feel swirling together,
the way her hips feel pressing against mine . . .

nothing but Sophie and me
and my hands gliding across her stomach . . .
my fingers bursting into flame
as they slide up under her T-shirt . . .

But before they even reach the bottom of her bra,

Sophie grabs my wrists, whispering, "No. Wait."
Then, she scoots away from me
to the other side of the bed—

the other side of the *world*.

A Few Seconds Later

She reaches for my hand,
saying, "I'm sorry, Robin."
"That's okay," I say.
Though my *body's* not so sure that it *is*.

My heart's still
thundering against my ribs
like a pissed-off prisoner
trying to break out of jail.

"It's just that it all felt so good," she says.
"Too good.
I've never felt that out of control before—
like I could just blink and end up pregnant."

"You can't get pregnant from blinking, silly," I say.
Then I wag my finger at her accusingly, and add,
"Someone hasn't been paying attention
in health class . . ."

Sophie laughs,
but a second later
she gets this real serious look on her face.
"I *want* to do more than just kiss you . . ." she says.

Whoa. She *does*?
My heart starts doing jumping jacks.
". . . But I've never done any of that stuff before.
So I need to take it slow. Okay?"

"Slow" wouldn't have been my first choice.

It wouldn't have even been my second choice.
In fact, "slow" isn't even on my *list*.
But "slow" is definitely better than "never."

So I say, "Sure, Sophie. There's no hurry."
And she flashes me a smile so devastating
that it could even make an *atheist*
believe in God.

I Do *Not* Have a One Track Mind

Yeah, right. Yeah, right. Yeah, right. Yeah,
right. Yeah, right. Yeah, right. Yeah, right. Yea
h, right. Yeah, right. Yeah, right. Yeah, right. Yeah,
right. Yeah, right. Yeah, right. Yeah, right. Yeah, right.
Yeah, right. Yeah, right. Yeah, right. Yeah, right. Yeah, rig
Yeah, right. **Yeah**, right. Yeah, right. Yeah, **right.** Yeah, right.
eah, right. Y**eah, righ**t. Yeah, right. Yeah, **right. Yeah**, right. Yea
right. Yeah, ri**ght. Y**eah, right. Y eah, right. Y**eah, ri**ght. Yeah, ri
ght. Yeah, right. Yeah, right. Y   eah, right. Yeah, right. Yeah,
right. Yeah, right. Yeah, rig   ht. Yeah, right. Yeah, righ
t. Yeah, right. Yeah, rig   ht. Yeah, right. Yeah,
right. Yeah, right.   Yeah, right. Yea

176

We Spend the Next Couple of Hours

Trying not to even *think* about sex.
Which is not an easy thing to do,
under the circumstances.

But we end up having a great time anyway,
looking through my stacks of *Weekly World News*,
and laughing at headlines like:

AGING BURGLAR
RIPS OFF OWN HOUSE BY MISTAKE.
And: MAN KILLS MIME AND NOBODY CARES.

We crack up over: HOW TO TELL IF
YOUR PROSTITUTE IS AN EXTRATERRESTRIAL.
And: ALIENS ARE HERE FOR OUR KRISPY KREMES.

Then we start cutting the headlines into bits and pieces,
rearranging them to create time-honored classics like:
HOW TO TELL IF YOUR KRISPY KREME IS A PROSTITUTE.

But some of the headlines are impossible to improve on.
Like this one, which we both agree is *très* hysterical as is:
POO LA LA! MAN SPEAKS FRENCH OUT OF HIS BUTT.

"Here's an intriguing one . . ." I say,
holding it up for Sophie to see:
TOUCHING BREASTS MAKES MEN LIVE LONGER.

She grabs the newspaper out of my hands and swats me.
"I predict you'll have a good life," she says,
"but a *short* one."

We Tack Our Best Creations Up onto My "Wall of Lame"

That's what I call the big wall next to my bed—
the one that I've covered
with all my favorite sketches and paintings,
plus cartoons and photos and funny postcards,
and tons of other miscellaneous weird-but-cool stuff.

"You're so lucky," Sophie says.
"My mom would never let me do this to *my* wall."
And, as if on cue, Sophie's cell starts ringing.
She checks the number and rolls her eyes.

"Speaking of my mom . . ." she grumbles. "Hello?
. . . Aw, come on, Mom . . . No!
You *can't* come yet . . . It's not even ten . . .
Can't you just . . . Can't I just—"
But Sophie's mom hangs up.

"*Sweet*," Sophie says,
glaring at the phone like she wants to murder it.
"She'll be here in ten minutes."
"Then we'd better make the best of them," I say.

Sophie wiggles her eyebrows at me lewdly
and says, "Great minds think alike."
And a second later,
we're practically kissing each other's
faces off.

Just Before Her Mom Arrives

Sophie and I make up a secret handshake.
It's more like a goof on secret handshakes—
because *this* one's actually
a footshake.

We start out
by walking toward each other
with our right hands stuck out in front of us,
like we are getting ready to shake.

Then, at the last second,
we reach down and grab hold
of the other person's right *ankle* instead,
shaking it in midair, as though it's a hand.

That probably sounds easier to do than it is.
But, really, it's pretty hard,
because the timing has to be perfect,
and both of us have to balance on one foot.

So the first few times that we try it,
we fall over on top of each other.
Which, of course,
is half the fun.

At School on Monday

Sophie and I meet by the water fountain
right before lunch.
Just like we planned.

We do our secret footshake, and crack up,
even though there are tons of people around,
staring at us like we're the scene of an accident.

But there's no way
we're gonna let them get to us.
So we just pull off our sweatshirts—

revealing that Sophie's wearing
her I AM *SUCH* A STEIN shirt,
and I'm wearing the one that says: I'M WITH STEIN.

Then I take hold of her hand
and we shove open the double doors to the cafeteria
like a couple of gunslingers entering a saloon.

As We Head Across the Room

And everyone reads
what it says on our shirts,
I'm not sure if a hush is falling over the crowd
or if it just *seems* that way.

A few people snicker.
But most of them
just stand there blinking at us,
like we're some kind of bizarre mirage.

When we pass by Zak and Danny and Henry,
they sneak these sidelong glances at each other,
like each one's scared to react until he finds out
what the *other* two guys are gonna do.

When Dylan reads the words on our shirts,
he looks like he wants
to say something real nasty to us,
only he's so stupid he can't come up with anything.

And when we walk past Rachel and Grace,
Grace looks like she wishes she could
fall right through the floor.
(Or like she wishes *Sophie and I* would.)

And Rachel looks like . . . like . . .
Well, I'm not exactly sure *what* she looks like.
So many different emotions are flashing across her face
that you'd have to be a speed-reader to catch them all.

When We Get to Our Usual Table

Sophie and I take out our lunch bags
and start joking around with each other,
trying to appear oblivious to the fact
that everyone's still staring.

And suddenly—
Rachel's standing right next to us!
She hesitates for a second,
then sits down on the bench beside Sophie.

She points across the table at me,
right at my I'M WITH STEIN shirt,
looks directly into my eyes,
and with this quivery-chinned little grin, says,

"*I am, too.*"

Whoa . . .

This must be
how the Red Sox felt

when the Curse of the Bambino

was finally
lifted.

Everyone's *Really* Staring at Us Now

So I usher Sophie and Rachel out of the cafeteria.

On our way to the door,
we walk right by the table where Grace is sitting,
her face looking whiter than a vampire's.

She's pretending not to see us,
but she's laughing real loud, *too* loud,
at something Henry's whispering in her ear.

I whisk the girls past her
and bring them over to Schultz's room,
so that they can make up with each other in private.

As soon as we get here,
I say good-bye and turn to leave.
But Rachel asks me to stay.

And a second later she bursts into tears
and starts apologizing.
To *both* of us.

Then Sophie's hugging Rachel,
and Rachel's hugging Sophie,
and both of them

are hugging *me*.

We Spend What's Left of the Lunch Period

Teaching Rachel the secret footshake,
writing I'M WITH STEIN on her T-shirt,
and drawing OUTLAWS RULE! tattoos
onto each other's arms.

And the entire time,
Rachel's filling Sophie in
on every single thing that's happened to her
in the last month.

Including the fact that at lunch today,
when Danny refused to come over to our table with her,
Rachel did something she'd been wanting to do
ever since winter break: she broke up with him.

Which, I've got to admit, is kind of impressive.
But even if it turned out
that Rachel was a complete ditz,
I still wouldn't mind chilling with her.

Because Sophie hasn't looked this happy in weeks.
She's lit up so bright
that it almost hurts my eyes to look at her.
Except that she's so beautiful,

I can't *keep* from looking at her.

Just Before the Bell Rings

Schultz walks in.
And when he finds us hanging out in his room,
he does this little double take.

But then he just grins at us,
saying, "Hey there, kiddos.
Glad to see you're making yourselves right at home."

And a second later,
when he reads what it says on all of our shirts,
he starts chuckling to himself, shaking his head.

"Brilliant . . ." he says.
"Where can *I* get one of those?"
So I grab a thick black marker off his desk

and say, "Allow me."

A Few Minutes Later

Rachel gives us the secret footshake
and rushes off to algebra.
Then, the rest of the people in Schultz's class
start trickling into the room.

When they see the words on Schultz's T-shirt,
some of them look confused,
some of them look uneasy,
but most of them look confused *and* uneasy.

Though these two girls we've never even talked to,
Bubba Shalhoub and Anita Fraker,
actually give Sophie and me little smiles of support
when they see what I've written on his shirt:

I AM *SUCH* A SCHULTZ.

Just as the Bell Rings

Zak slinks in.
And when he reads Schultz's shirt,
his eyes pop a little.

Schultz just stands there in front of the class,
sort of rocking back and forth on his heels,
looking at us with this mischievous gleam in his eye.

Then he says,
"How do you like
my new shirt, kiddos?"

There's a few seconds of total silence,
until Zak finally says,
"It sucks, Mr. S."

And the really weird thing is:
not a single person laughs
when he says this.

Schultz pushes out his lower lip.
"Oh, dear me," he says.
"Now you've gone and hurt my feelings."

At which point,
everyone *does* laugh.
Except for Zak.

Schultz Strikes Again

He puts on this old CD
of Coleman Hawkins wailing out
this ancient jazz on tenor sax,
then tells us all to close our eyes
and listen for a while.

A few kids groan,
but pretty soon they quiet down,
and then there's just this lazy sound
of breathy riffs that wind themselves
around the tinkling of piano keys . . .

It may not be old rock and roll,
but this stuff's cool in *other* ways—
cool in *hot* ways, sexy ways,
that make me think of Sophie
under satin sheets . . .

of both of us
with no clothes on,
together in a darkened room,
alone and pressing
skin to skin . . .

"And now, for today's assignment,"
Schultz's voice breaks in.
"I want all of you to keep listening to the music,
then draw what it's making you see."
What it's making me *see*?!

Dude.
I'm screwed.

It's 3:23 p.m.

And I've been standing here
waiting by the goalpost,
with my heart beating faster every minute.
Sophie's never been this late before.
What if something awful's happened to her?

Then finally,
she bursts through the back door of the building.
But she's not alone—
Rachel's with her.

And as I watch them heading toward me,
laughing and leaning in
to share some little secret,
this sinking feeling grabs hold of my stomach.

Because the whole afternoon,
all I could think about was how much
I wanted to celebrate with Sophie,
and how I could hardly wait to be alone with her—

so I could talk to her about
all the amazing things that happened to us today,
so I could grab her and kiss her
and wrap myself around her . . .
But I can't do *any* of that stuff

in front of Rachel.

Which Totally Sucks

And, as if that isn't bad enough,
Sophie says she hopes I don't mind,
but she promised Rachel we'd help her
with her psychology project this afternoon:

which is to go trick-or-treating
(even though it's *February*)
and then use a hidden video camera
to record how people react.

Rachel makes Sophie and me dress up as the parents,
in these real tacky middle-aged clothes.
And *she* dresses up as our daughter,
in this puffy pink dress and a sparkly tiara.

Then, we go out into the neighborhood,
and before we ring the bell each time,
Rachel gets down on her knees,
hiding her legs underneath her skirt.

So that when the people open their doors,
she looks sort of like a teenager
who's pretending to be a little kid
who's pretending to be a princess.

And I kind of hate to admit it,
but when Rachel smiles up at them,
holds out her paper bag, and shouts, "Trick or treat!"
the expressions that the people get on their faces

are pretty hilarious.

But Later

When we go over to Rachel's house
to watch the footage we shot with the hidden camera,
that sinking feeling grabs hold of my stomach again,
even tighter than it did before.

Because just when I'm getting ready
to snuggle up to Sophie on the couch,
Rachel plunks herself down
right *between* us.

And the thing is,
Sophie doesn't even seem to notice.
Or if she *does*,
she sure doesn't seem to mind.

But what really gets to me
is what happens when we finish watching the video
and I offer to walk Sophie home,
hoping for at least a *few* minutes alone with her.

Because that's when Sophie
just smiles over at Rachel,
like they've got lots of catching up to do,
and says I should go on home

without her.

Sophie Gives Me a Sisterly Peck
on the Cheek Good-bye

And I trudge off through the aching cold
of the subzero dusk,

feeling way sorry for myself.
And way confused.

I mean,
what is wrong with me, anyway?

I've spent the entire last month
wishing that Sophie could have her old friends back.

But now that she and Rachel
have been reunited,

I can't help wishing that things could be
the way they were *before*,

when it was just Sophie
and me against the world—

and outlaws ruled . . .

Right After Dinner

I dialed Sophie's cell.
I don't really know why.
I guess I just wanted
to hear her voice.

"Robin!" she said,
like she was real happy to hear from me.
Like she had no idea
that anything was even bothering me.

"You got a minute to talk?" I said.
"Oops. Wait a sec," she said,
"I'm getting another call."
Then she put me on hold.

A second later, she got back on the line.
"It's Rachel," she said.
"I'll call you *right* back."
Then she clicked off.

That was an hour ago.

So When I Head Over to Studio B

I'm feeling sort of like the Forgotten Man.

I arrive a little early, but Tessa's already here.
She grins at me and flashes the peace sign.
"Hey, Rockin' Robin," she says, "feelin' groovy?"

"Oh, you know," I say. "Could be better."
"I'm sorry to hear that," Tessa says.
And she looks like she really *is*.

"Maybe a pop quiz will cheer you up," she says,
giving me a friendly little squeeze.
"Who was the lead singer of the Troggs?"

I hesitate for a second,
while Tessa sucks in her breath
and crosses her fingers.

Then I fold my arms over my chest
and start shaking my head,
trying my best to look irritatingly smug.

"Aw, that's too easy," I say.
"It was Chip Taylor."
(Even though I know *full well* it was Reg Presley.)

And when I see the smile
that's spreading across Tessa's face,
sort of like the sun coming out after an eclipse,

I *do* feel a little bit better.

Chelsea's Back!

But I guess I must be getting used to
staring at fantastic-looking naked women
with unbelievably creamy skin and perfect breasts
who are standing only a few feet away from me.

Because even though she looks,
if anything,
even hotter than she did
the first time she modeled for us,

this time, for some unknown reason,
I'm able to concentrate on *drawing* her,
instead of just concentrating
on how staggeringly sexy she is.

This time I can actually look at her butt
and see it as a form
that's defined by areas of light and shadow,
instead of as a form defined by areas

that I wish I could get my hands on.

Tuesday Morning

I'd planned on saying something snide
when I saw Sophie.
You know—
like I'd pull my cell phone out of my pocket,
and say something like:

"Oh. Hey.
How you doing?
I'm still waiting for you
to call me *right* back . . ."

But when she and Rachel run up to me in the hall,
and I see that Rachel's wearing a T-shirt that says:
ANY FRIEND OF STEIN
IS A FRIEND OF MINE,
it sort of takes the wind out of my sails.

This Is So Messed Up

Shouldn't I
be feeling
a heck of a lot better
right now?

I mean, some people we don't even *know*
came up to Sophie and me in the cafeteria today
and asked us if we'd teach them how
to do "that funny foot-shaking thing."

Then,
when Dylan performed
his daily hat-grabbing ritual,
not a single goon cheered him on.

And a minute ago,
Sophie rushed up to me and told me
that when she walked into math class,
Grace actually made eye contact with her.

She said for a second there
Grace almost sort of looked like
she was getting ready to smile at her.
Only then she didn't.

Sophie said she knows it's a real long shot,
but she's hoping that maybe
if we give Grace a little more time
she might even come over to our side.

So,
shouldn't I be over the moon?

Tap-dancing on the ceiling?
Doing handsprings or something?

Then how come I'm not?
And how come my life feels like
it's about a hundred times more complicated
than a quadratic equation?

I'm Waiting by the Goalpost

Hoping that *this* time
when Sophie comes to me,
she'll be alone.

Because it's been so long since I've kissed her,
I mean *really* kissed her,
that I'm practically going into withdrawal.

But when she finally pushes through the back door,
and starts running across the field to me,
Rachel's trotting along right next to her.

And a minute later,
when they get to the goalpost,
Sophie doesn't even kiss me on the cheek.

She just tells me that there's
this amazing sale on at Bloomingdale's,
and that it just started this morning.

"Sophie has to come *with* me," Rachel says,
"My mom's so worried about perverts abducting me
that she won't let me cruise the mall alone."

"I won't go, though," Sophie says,
"if you don't want me to."
But her eyes plead with mine: *Don't ask me to stay* . . .

So I force myself to say, "That's okay."
Then she hugs me, thanks me,
and runs away.

For a Long Time

I keep my eyes trained
on the back of Sophie's head,

willing her
to glance over her shoulder,

willing her to turn around
and run back to me,

willing her
to fling her arms around my neck

and give me
a passionate kiss good-bye . . .

but she just keeps
right on going.

I Try to Tell Myself

That Sophie doesn't *mean*
to be neglecting me.

That the only reason
she's been so distracted lately

is because she's so happy
that Rachel's back in her life.

And *I'm* happy *for* her.
I really am.

It's just that, until now,
I never realized

how sad
being happy

could make a guy
feel.

I've Survived Dinner with My Prying Parents

Now I'm trying to concentrate
on studying for my math test.
But all I can think about is
Sophie. So I'm just sitting
here, staring at my computer
screen, zooming all the way in from outer space, all the
way down to America, then down to Massachusetts,
and all the way to Cambridge, zooming past the
ribbon of the Charles, and all the way down
to Shepard Street, down and down and
down, till I find Sophie's house . . . And if
the camera could keep on zooming,
right through an open window
and go *inside* that house,
I'd be able to see the girl
who's forgotten I exist,
the girl I haven't
kissed since
yester-
day.

I Drag Myself Out of Bed on Wednesday Morning

And trudge to school,
with my heart just sitting in my chest,
as heavy and lifeless as a paperweight.

But then I catch sight of Sophie—
waiting for me
right outside the door to my health class!

And when she sees me,
she rushes up to me
and throws her arms around my neck.

"I brought you something," she says.
"Something I forgot to give you yesterday."
And then—she kisses me.

When we finally pull apart,
I say, "I brought *you* something, too."
And then *I* kiss *her*, which makes both of us laugh.

"I've got lots more where that came from," I say,
"if you want to come over after school and get some.
We could hang out. Just the two of us."

"I'd *love* that . . ." she says.
And when the bell rings a second later,
and she hurries off around the corner,

I pump my fist in the air,
and whisper,
"*Yes!*"

Maybe There's Hope for My Love Life

Maybe
there's even some hope
for my school life.

Because all morning long,
these real mind-boggling things
keep happening.

Like when I see
a couple of jocks in my health class
doing the secret footshake.

And when this total prom-queen type
comes up to me in math class .
to show me her OUTLAWS RULE! tattoo.

I'm feeling so good,
that it doesn't even bother me
when I see Dylan walking down the hall—

wearing a T-shirt with a crudely drawn picture
of a two-headed monster on it,
and just one word scrawled below it:

MURPHENSTEIN.

I'm Still Kind of Dreading Lunch, Though

Dreading having to share Sophie
with Rachel.

But she's a *package* deal now.
Why can't I just accept that?

I mean, if I want *her*,
I've got to take Rachel right along with her.

Besides, this is what
I've been wishing for all along, isn't it?

For Sophie to get back together
with her old friends.

So how come
my throat gets so tight

when she comes bopping up to me
outside the cafeteria

with Rachel glued to her side
like some kind of Siamese twin?

But Lunch Isn't That Bad, Really

Once I get used to
having to eat with *two* people
instead of one,

two people who've known each other
for such a long time
that they practically speak in code,

two people who are always saying,
"Remember the time when *this* happened?"
and "Remember the time when *that* happened?"

(Which, of course,
I never do,
because I wasn't there.)

Well, okay—
it *is* that bad.
It sucks, even.

But if I can just make it through
to the end of the day,
I'll finally have Sophie

all to myself.

When She Runs Up to Me at the Goalpost

Our mouths are drawn together
like two supercharged magnets.

And we get so carried away,
so fast,

that we just barely
manage

to stop making out
long enough

to race over
to my house

and *start*
making out.

As Soon as We Get Upstairs to My Room

It's like there's
no future,

no
past,

only
now.

Right
now.

The greatest
now

I've ever
known.

Only
now—

this
kiss,

this
wow!

Then, Without Any Warning

Sophie's cell starts ringing!
Jolting us
out of the spell we were under.

We try to ignore it for a while,
but our kisses start fizzling,
then stop altogether.

Both of us groan
as Sophie yanks herself out of my arms
to dig her phone out of her backpack.

Only the thing is,
when she finally gets her hands on it,
she doesn't switch it off—

she *answers* it.

Guess Who's Calling?

But Sophie isn't telling her
that she'll have to talk to her later.
She isn't hurrying to hang up the phone
and throw herself back into my arms.

She's just pressing it to her ear,
listening intently,
with her eyes getting bigger by the second,
oblivious to the fact
that she's totally ignoring me.

"Omigod . . . omi*god!*" she says. "I'd love to!
But are you sure it's okay with your parents?"

Sophie keeps her ear welded to the phone,
hanging on Rachel's every word,
completely forgetting that I'm even sitting here—
sitting here fuming,
waiting for her to hang up the freaking phone.

Then she says, "No way . . . no *way!*
You mean my mom already said I can *go*?
I can't believe this.
I can't *believe* it!"

"That makes two of us," I growl under my breath.

I Sit and Seethe

Listening to Sophie jabber on and on and on.
And when she finally *does* hang up,
she's got so many stars in her eyes
that she doesn't seem to notice the daggers in *mine*.

She leaps off the bed
and starts dancing around the room,
telling me that Rachel's taking her to Bermuda
with her family this weekend.

"I never get to go *any*where.
And now I'm going to the Caribbean
to stay in a fancy condo right on the beach!
Isn't that amazing?"

"Yeah," I say. "It *is* amazing.
Amazing that you'd rather
talk on the phone to Rachel
than make out with *me*."

That's when the stars in Sophie's eyes
disappear behind a cloud bank.
"Wait a minute, Robin," she says,
"that's not true. I—"

"Yup," I say. "It's pretty amazing, all right.
Amazing that my own girlfriend
couldn't care less that she's gonna
be away from me all weekend."

Sophie's eyes fill with tears.
"I thought you'd be happy for me," she says,

making herself sound all pathetic.
"Well, I'm *not!*" I shout.

And my words reverberate
in the sudden silence,
like the slamming
of a door.

Sophie's Cheeks Look as Red as if I'd Slapped Them

"I'd be happy for *you*," she says,
in a voice as quiet as the eye of a hurricane,
"even though you obviously don't care about
anyone but your*self.*"

"Look who's talking!" I say.
"I wasn't expecting you to turn down Bermuda.
But you could have at least *pretended* to feel
a little bit sad about going away without me."

"And *you* could have at least pretended
to be a little understanding about it," she says,
"considering that it's *your* fault
I haven't seen Rachel practically all winter!"

That hits me like a blow below the belt.
And suddenly, it's like we're having a fistfight,
only instead of flinging punches,
we're flinging words at each other.

And a few minutes later,
when Sophie stomps down the stairs
and storms out the door,
I'm literally hopping mad.

I mean,
like I'm actually jumping up and down,
pounding the air,
screaming at the empty hallway.

Later

When I get to my drawing class,
I'm still so pissed at Sophie
that my heart's clenched in my chest
like a lead fist.

There's a new model tonight—a milk-skinned goth
with more piercings than a pincushion,
and a shiny snake of pink-and-black-striped braid,
swirling down her back like a question mark,

a question mark
that reminds me
that I still don't have any answers
to some very pressing questions.

Like what is *wrong* with Sophie, anyway?
How come ever since she started
hanging around with Rachel
she's been acting like an entirely different person?

Felix tells us to be archaeologists,
to dig deep into the paper.
"Scratch it," he says. "Gouge it.
Run over it with your mopeds."

Which is exactly
what I'm in the mood to do.
Only I was thinking more along the lines
of a Mack truck.

My Charcoal's on a Rampage

Tearing into the paper
like a bull ripping into a matador's cape.

This isn't just a drawing,
it's a brawl—

a knock-down drag-out
free-for-all.

I smear it, smudge it,
wrinkle it, tear it,

scrawl all my rage out
onto the page.

During the Break

When Honk comes over
to check out what I've done,
he lets out a low whistle.

When Richard sees it,
he gasps and ducks behind Eve
for cover.

Eve makes the sign of the cross with her fingers,
like people do in the movies
when they're trying to ward off vampires.

But Tessa just grins at me
and says, "Feel better now?"
And I have to admit—I *do*.

At Finale

The five of us are tucked into a dimly lit booth,
licking the last crumbs
of Dark Chocolate Decadence off our forks,

when I happen to notice
that my left thigh is pressed against Eve's thigh,
and my right one is pressed against Tessa's.

This causes me
to have an impure thought.
A *couple* of impure thoughts, actually.

I can feel the heat
from both of their legs
penetrating right through my jeans.

Did the girls press *their* thighs
against *mine*?
Or did *I* press *mine* against *theirs*?

Is it possible
that they could be
flirting with me?

And, right at that moment, as if both girls
heard me ask my question out loud,
each of them shifts her leg against mine,

applying just a little more pressure.

Of Course, I'm Probably Only Imagining This

But real or imagined, it's turning me on.
And I find myself wishing I could slip a hand
onto each of their thighs and—

That's when I realize that Eve is talking to me.
"So," she's saying,
"are you up for doing it with us, Robin?"

"Up for . . . *doing* it with you?"
My heart starts thumping in my chest
like I'm running the Boston Marathon.

"Please," Tessa says, "I *need* you."
Gulp.
"You . . . do?"

"Sure she does, bro," Honk says. "Tessa needs
all *four* of us to chill with her on Saturday
and help her celebrate her birthday in *style.*"

Tessa's birthday?
That's what they were
talking about?

"So, are you gonna grace us
with your illustrious presence?"
Richard says.

"I wouldn't miss it," I say.

It Isn't Until a While Later

After we all exchange cell numbers
so we can firm up
the plans for Saturday,

after Tessa leans her head against my shoulder
and tells me how glad she is
that I'll be with her on her birthday,

after I sling an arm
over each of the girls' shoulders
and give them both a squeeze,

that I start thinking about Sophie,
thinking about how she'd feel
if she could see me right now,

thinking that it would
serve her
right!

On Thursday

I spend the whole morning
doing whatever I can
to keep from bumping into Sophie at school.

I even sneak upstairs to the second floor
to get from my health class to math class,
just so I'll be sure not to run into her.

Except I *do* run into her.
Because Sophie's up here, too.
She must have had the exact same idea.

And when our eyes meet,
I look away so fast
that I almost get whiplash.

During lunch,
I hole up in Schultz's room,
avoiding the cafeteria completely.

And after lunch, when Sophie
walks into the room for art class,
both of us act like the other person

is invisible.

When I Get Home After School

I find my mom cramming clothes into the dryer,
with her hair wrapped up in a towel.
"How come you're home so early, Mom?"

"Well," she says, heaving an exhausted sigh,
"first you have to promise me
you won't shoot the messenger."

But before she can explain what she means by this,
my dad staggers into the room,
carrying a pile of laundry that's taller than he is.

Uh-oh.
His hair's wrapped up in a towel, too!
"Oh, no . . ." I say, "not *again*."

Right away,
my scalp starts itching like crazy.
And so does my beard.

"Yep," she says. "Second time this year—
your father and I just found out
that both of us have lice."

"And so, apparently,
do half the kids at Happy Time," Dad says,
dumping an avalanche of laundry onto the floor.

"But we're thinking of changing the name,"
Mom says with a grim little chuckle,
"to *Un*happy Time."

My Heart's Trying Real Hard

To exit my body through my throat right now.
Because my dad's checking my beard and my scalp
to see if I've got lice.

And if I *do*,
then I'll have to inform Sophie.
Since those nasty little bugs could have easily
jumped right off of *me* onto *her*.

I can picture the whole excruciating scene:
"Sophie," I'll begin, "I know we aren't exactly
on speaking terms right now,
but there's something I need to tell you . . ."

"Oh, just go ahead and spit it out, Robin," she'll hiss.
So I'll brace myself and continue.
"Okay, then. You know the other day,
when we were making out on my bed?"

And Sophie won't say anything,
but she'll sort of shudder,
like she can't believe
she ever *wanted* to make out with me.

"Well . . ." I'll say,
"we weren't quite
as *alone* in that bed

as we thought we were . . ."

I've Been Spared!

Dad's just pronounced my entire head
a "louse-free zone"!

"Thank *God!*" Mom says.
"But be careful not to touch anything, Robin.
The house is probably still crawling with them."

Then she shivers convulsively,
turning to my dad
with this wild sort of gleam in her eye.

"And it must be ten times worse at the school.
You've got to get over there right now
and bag up all the things from the dress-up center."

"I do?" he asks wearily.
"Yes! *Please!*" Mom says. "Every scrap of it!"

"Don't worry," Dad says,
trudging toward the door.
"There'll be no tutu, no cape, no hat left behind."

"And watch out how you handle that stuff,"
she calls after him. "It must be positively infested.
Especially those hats."

And just thinking about the hats,
with all those lice running rampant all over them,
sends a chill down my spine—

and gives me one of the best ideas
I've ever had in my life.

So I Wait Until My Mom Takes a Martini Break

(She's not much of a drinker,
but I guess today's an exception.)

Then,
like a skilled criminal mastermind,
I set my plan into motion:

I pull on a pair of plastic gloves
and start searching through
the lice-infested laundry pile.

I'm looking for my dad's Red Sox cap—
the one he's worn every single day
since they won the World Series.

And when I finally find it,
I slip it into a jumbo Ziploc bag
and sneak it upstairs to my room,

where I take off my own hat,
put it into the bag right on top of my dad's cap,
and zip them up together, real tight.

Then I toss back my head
and shout, "Mwa-ha-ha-ha!"

And Suddenly I'm Thinking About Sophie

Thinking about how much she'd love this plan,
and about how much more fun
this whole thing would be
if *she* were doing it
with me . . .

And for a minute there,
I get this real strong urge to call her—
to just call her up
and act like nothing's happened
and ask her if she wants
to help me execute my plan.

But then I remember
all the awful stuff she said to me,
and all the awful stuff
I said to *her*,
and the urge

passes.

On Friday Morning

I sneak my dad's cap back down
into the laundry room.
Then I zip up the bag with my own hat still in it,
and hide it inside my backpack.

I feel sort of naked
heading out of the house
with a bare head,
but it's all for an evil cause.

When I get to school, my thoughts shift to Sophie—
maybe she'll be waiting for me
outside of health class,
like she was the other day.

Maybe she'll
throw her arms around my neck
and kiss me
and tell me how sorry she is.

Maybe she'll tell me
that she's decided not to even *go* to Bermuda,
that she'd rather stay home
and spend the weekend with *me*.

Then again,
maybe she won't.
Because I can see the door to my classroom now,
and Sophie isn't anywhere near it.

It's Basically the Same Drill as Thursday

Sophie and I try to avoid each other all day.
And when avoiding each other can't be avoided,
we try not to look at each other.

The only time my mood improves
is right before English,
when I see Dylan waiting to pounce on me.

I make sure he's looking right at me,
then I slip my hat out of its plastic bag
and shove it behind my back
like I'm trying to hide it.

Dylan makes a beeline for me and says,
"Hey, Murphy. Where's that wicked cool hat of yours?"
I pretend to be caught off guard by his question.
"Um . . . uh . . . at the cleaner's?" I say.

"For chrissake," he says, reaching behind me
and grabbing it out of my hand.
"How dumb do you think I *am*?"
But I don't think it'd be a good idea
to answer that particular question right now.

So I don't say anything.
I just lunge for my hat,
trying my best to make it *look* like
I really want to get it away from him.

"Whatsa matter, Murphy?" he says,
yanking it out of my reach

and smashing it down onto his *own* head.
"Afraid you're gonna get my cooties?"

I recoil with what I hope looks like actual horror.
"Take it off!" I shout, lunging for it again.
But that only makes him press it down
onto his own head even tighter.

Darn.

I Keep Trying to Snatch My Hat Back

Until the bell rings.
Then I beg Dylan not to throw it out the window.
So, of course—he *does*.

This allows me to run outside
and slip it safely back into its plastic bag
without being seen.

I'll be late to English class,
but if my mission's been accomplished,
it will have been *way* worth it.

Now,
I'll just have to wait a day or two
and see what happens . . .

Late on Friday Night

I'm sitting at my computer,
messing around on Google Earth,
cruising through the streets of Bermuda,
thinking about Sophie,

wondering which one of these streets
she's on right now,
wondering if maybe
she's thinking about *me*, too . . .

Probably not—
probably
I'm the furthest thing
from her mind.

But maybe,
if I concentrate real hard on her,
she'll be able to sense it,
be able to pick up on my vibe . . .

Sophie's always saying
she *knows* things.
Maybe she'll know
I'm thinking about her . . .

I close my eyes,
trying to picture her face.
And the second I *do*—
my cell rings!

I Grab the Phone

"Sophie!" I say. "It's you!"

But there's a silence on the other end.
"Uh . . . no," a voice says. "It's Tessa, actually."
"Tessa? . . . Oh. *Tessa.* Hi!" I say. "Sorry about that.
I was expecting another call."

"Let me guess . . ." she says with a little laugh.
"From Sophie, right?"
"Yeah. She's my . . .
she's a friend of mine," I say.

And as soon as these words
pop out of my mouth,
I wonder why I didn't tell her
that Sophie's my girlfriend.

Maybe it's because
I'm not even sure
Sophie *wants* to be my girlfriend
anymore . . .

Tessa Says She's Calling to Tell Me the Plan

"We're all meeting in the Yard
by the statue of John Harvard
tomorrow morning at seven thirty, okay?"
"*Seven thirty*?" I say. "That is *not* okay!"

"I know, I know," she says.
"I thought seven thirty in the morning
was just a nasty rumor.
But apparently it actually exists."

Then she says that Richard's insisting
we start off her birthday celebration
by witnessing "an undisclosed sociological event."
And he says we'll miss it if we aren't there by eight.

"Seven thirty's fine," I say. "I was only kidding.
I'm used to getting up early."
Though, of course, I don't tell her the reason *why*—
which is that I'm still just in high school.

As soon as we say good-bye,
my focus shifts back
to the virtual streets of Bermuda.
And to Sophie.

"Well, what did you *expect* me to do
while you were gone?" I say to the screen.
"Sit here in my room all weekend,
twiddling my thumbs?"

Richard's "Undisclosed Sociological Event"

Turns out to be
the Running of the Brides,
this huge annual wedding-dress sale
that they have at Filene's Basement.

We get there just as the doors swing open
and hundreds of screaming brides
run into the store,
along with their screaming mothers
and all their screaming bridesmaids.

It's like some kind of crazy extreme sport.
The dress racks are stripped bare
sixty seconds after the stampede of shoppers attacks.
And that's not the only thing that's stripped bare.

The frenzied brides-to-be have all peeled
down to their underwear to try on the gowns!
Tessa and Eve put their hands over our eyes
so that we can't ogle the customers.

Then Eve helps Tessa try on one of the dresses.
And when Tessa takes off her T-shirt
and slips the dress on over her tank top and jeans
she looks sort of . . .
well, I guess she looks kind of beautiful.

Which is pretty weird.
Because until this minute,
I hadn't ever noticed that about her.
That she's beautiful, I mean.

Honk Performs an Impromptu Wedding

Randomly grabbing Richard
to unite him in unholy matrimony with Tessa.
Then Eve and I pelt the newlyweds with Skittles,
since we don't have any rice.

After that,
we head over to Little Italy for some breakfast,
laughing when Tessa starts feeding Richard
all these big sloppy bites of cannoli,
like a bride feeding wedding cake to her groom.

From there,
I suggest we hit the Museum of Dirt.
"Because I know that Tessa
will really *dig* it," I say.

Everyone groans at my pun.
But they flip when we actually get here
and start looking at the labels
on all the little glass bottles.

"Whoa . . ." Richard says. "Donner Party dirt!"
"Check it . . ." Eve says.
"This dirt's from Martha Stewart's compost heap!"
"And look at this . . ." Honk says.
"Dirt from Diana's crash site!"

Though Tessa's the most stoked of all.
She nearly faints when I show her
the dirt from Mick Jagger's flower bed.

But when she sees the dirt from Graceland,
she throws her arms around my neck
and tells Richard she's filing for divorce—
so that she can marry a man
who *truly* understands her:

me.

Then, Eve Suggests We Bypass Lunch

And instead, she takes us to
the Chocolate Bar at Café Fleuri,
an all-you-can-eat chocolate buffet.

We gorge on chocolate mousse,
chocolate truffles, chocolate ice cream,
chocolate cakes,

chocolate pies,
chocolate cookies, chocolate pudding,
chocolate crepes . . .

We even try chocolate sushi,
chocolate chicken, chocolate pizza,
and chocolate soup . . .

And when we've eaten ourselves sick,
and we're all just sitting around
going into sugar shock,

I say, "Hey. Maybe if we tell the waiter
that it's Tessa's birthday,
he'll give her a free dessert."

Everyone cracks up,
and just then, for some unknown reason,
I happen to glance toward the door.

And guess who's walking through it?
Dylan!
Flanked by his parents.

He doesn't see me,
but I see *him.*
And a huge grin spreads across my face—

because I can't help noticing
that he's scratching his head
like a wild man.

Feeling Triumphant

I rouse everyone
out of their chocolate-induced stupors
and take them over
to the Mapparium.

It's hard to explain what this place is like,
but try to imagine being on the inside looking out
of a three-story-tall stained-glass globe
of the world.

When we walk out onto
the suspended glass bridge
that runs right through the center of it,
we notice that there's an amazing echo in here.

So we gather round Tessa
and sing her "Happy Birthday."
The acoustics are so spectacular
that we practically sound like a chorus of angels.

When we're finished, Tessa says,
"Thanks, guys.
That was awesome.
This whole *day's* been awesome."

"I guess you're just about the luckiest
birthday girl in the world," I say.
"*In* the *world*. Get it?"
Tessa laughs and rolls her eyes at my pun.

Then she gives me a hug

and I give her one back.
And just at that exact moment, I happen to
glance up at the map of the world overhead,

and my eyes land right on Bermuda.

When We Get Back to Harvard at Around Six

No one's ready for the party to be over.

So Tessa invites all of us
up to her suite in the dorm.
It's set up kind of like a hotel suite,
with a living room she calls a common room,
and some bedrooms off a hallway to the left.

Tessa, Richard, Eve, and I
flop down on the couches
in the common room.
But Honk rushes out the door,
saying he'll be right back.

A few minutes later, he returns
with a platter full of all these ice-cube-size
chunks of strawberry Jell-O.
"Snack time!" he says.

Everyone seems real pleased to see this Jell-O,
which strikes me as a little bit weird.
But I'm not exactly up on my college crazes.
Maybe Jell-O's all the rage right now . . .

"To Tessa!" Honk says,
holding up the jiggling red cube in his hand
like it's a glass of champagne.
"On her . . . on her . . . how old *are* you, anyway, Tessa?"

"I'm . . . I'm only . . . eighteen," she says,
like she's not real crazy about admitting it.
"A mere baby," Richard says.

"To baby Tessa," Eve says,
"on her eighteenth birthday!"

"To Tessa!" we all say.
Then we "clink" our Jell-O cubes together
and toss them back like shots of whiskey.
"Geez," I think to myself.
"If they think *she's* a baby . . ."

Then Richard Asks for Some Tunes

So I figure now would be a good time
to give Tessa the present I made for her last night—
a mix of birthday-themed rock and roll oldies.

It's got classics,
like the Beatles' "Birthday" song,
and Lesley Gore singing "It's My Party."

And some funny stuff too,
like this weird old track I found of some dogs
barking out the tune of "Happy Birthday."

Tessa loves it.
And so does everyone else.
We all get up and start dancing.

And that's when I notice
that I feel strangely loose,
like all my joints

have been oiled.

We Don't Stop Rocking Out

Till Chuck Berry finishes singing
"Sweet Little Sixteen."
Then we flop back down on the couches
and Honk offers us some more Jell-O.

All that dancing made me so hot,
and the Jell-O feels so nice and cool
sliding down my throat,
that I help myself to a third chunk of it.

"You're so lucky you live in Grays,"
Eve says to Tessa.
"Your common room's big enough
for a dance party."

"You're living in the Harvard Hilton," Honk says.
And then, without any warning,
Richard turns to me and asks,
"Which dorm do *you* live in, Robin?"

"I . . . uh . . . I . . ." I mumble, trying to think of a way
to avoid answering the question.
But the hard drive in my head
seems to have crashed.

And all of a sudden it hits me how tired I am—
tired of always having to pretend
to be someone I'm not.
So I just blurt it out:

"I don't go to Harvard."

For a Few Seconds, No One Says Anything

Then Eve breaks the silence.
"I *knew* it!" she says.
You're an M.I.T. man, aren't you?"

"What? No, I—"
"Hold on a minute," Richard says.
"Let *me* have a shot at this: Boston College, right?"

"No. *No.* I go to—"
"Wait. *I* know," Honk says.
"It's Brandeis, isn't it?"

I open my mouth to speak,
but I can't seem to form a sentence.
So I just shake my head no.

"Where *do* you go, Robin?" Tessa finally says,
staring at me with wide, curious eyes.
I take a deep breath and force the words out:

"To high school."

My Words Hang in the Air

Like a grenade with its pin pulled out.
I grit my teeth
and wait for the explosion . . .

Tessa blinks at me in disbelief.
Here it comes . . .
Here it comes . . .

But then she just grins and says,
"That's so cool.
What grade are you in?"

Huh?
Did she just use the word "cool" to describe
the fact that I'm still in high school?

"I'm . . . I'm a freshman," I say.
Honk's eyebrows shoot up.
"So that means you're only, what—fourteen?"

"Fourteen and three quarters, actually."
And when they all burst out laughing,
it dawns on me

how totally infantile that must have sounded.

But Then Honk High-Fives Me

"You're an amazing artist, bro," he says,
"for someone so young."
"He's an amazing artist, period," Tessa says.
"And an amazing *con* artist," Richard says,
slapping me on the back.

"We've been punked," Honk says.
"It must have been his beard," Eve says.
"It makes him look so . . . so grown *up*."
"And so *hot*," Tessa says,
giggling and snuggling up to me.

I swallow hard,
and that's when I realize how thirsty I am.
So I slip another chunk of Jell-O down my throat.
Which is when Richard gasps and says,
"Omigod! We've been corrupting a minor!"

"What are you talking about?" I say.
"These are Jell-O shots," Tessa says.
"There's vodka in them."
"Ohhhh . . ." I say, pondering this new
piece of information.

"Then that would explain why I'm so *wasted*."

After the Last Jell-O Shot Kicks In

Time shifts into this weird kind of warp,
where everything's happening real fast,
but in this strange slow-motiony sort of way . . .

And when I glance around the room,
I notice that Richard's asleep
on one of the couches.

And that—whoa . . .
Eve and Honk
are making out on the other one!

Tessa rolls her eyes,
motioning to the kissing couple.
"I think they need some privacy," she whispers.

Then she takes hold of my hand
and leads me down a short hallway,
mumbling, "Let's get out of here."

My head feels like a balloon,
bobbing above the rest of me
like it's attached to my body by a thread.

I'm so dizzy that I have to lean against Tessa
to keep from falling over.
"Where are we going?" I say.

"To *my* room," she says.

We Flop Down onto Tessa's Bed

And just lie here on our backs,
staring up at the ceiling
with the room spinning around us
and the bed sort of floating . . .

Then Roy Orbison starts singing
"Sixteen Candles,"
and, out of the blue,
Tessa turns to me and says,

"You want to know a secret?"
"Sure."
"Promise you won't tell?"
"I promise."

But she hesitates, like she's still not sure
she should go through with it.
Then she squeezes her eyes closed and says it:
"I'm not really eighteen—I'm *six*teen."

Geez . . . it's lucky I'm already lying down,
or I probably would have fallen over just now.
I thought *I* was the only one
hiding something.

I grin at her and say, "That's so great.
You mean you're just a year older than me?"
"Well," she says,
"a year and a quarter, actually."

And both of us crack up.

But a Second Later, Tessa Stops Laughing

"Hey, wait a minute," she says.
"How come you lied to us about your age?"
"I didn't lie," I protest. "You just never asked me."
Then I say, "How come *you* lied?"

Tessa gets this real serious look on her face.
"Because if word gets out about how young I am,
none of the guys at Harvard
will want to go out with me."

"You think?" I say.
"I *know*," she says.
"That's been the pathetic story
of my pathetically nonexistent love life—

I skipped so many grades,
that by the time I got to high school,
I was three years younger than all the boys.
Three years younger and twice as smart.

Which is *not* a big turn-on for your average guy."

Then Neil Sedaka Starts Singing "Happy Birthday, Sweet Sixteen"

Tessa looks into my eyes, bites her lower lip,
and says, "Okay. Pop quiz:
Which rock-and-roll-obsessed Harvard freshman
is sweet sixteen and never been kissed?"

She doesn't mean
what I *think* she means, does she?
"Uh . . ." I say.
". . . I give up. Which one?"

Tessa's cheeks flush pink,
but she doesn't say anything.
She just points
her finger

at herself.

And Then

Before I even realize what I'm saying,
I'm telling her not to worry about it,

telling her
that we can solve that problem right now.

And then I'm leaning in—
and I'm kissing her!

And her lips feel so hungry on mine . . .
so hungry and so hot . . .

And we're kissing
and kissing and kissing . . .

drifting away
on an ocean of kisses . . .

and without any warning
Tessa takes hold of my hands

and slides them right up
underneath her shirt!

I'm Touching Her Breasts!

Actually touching
a girl's breasts!

I can't believe this is happening.
It's too good to be true.

I'm finally doing
what I've wanted to do,

what I've ached to do
for so long.

This
feels amazing . . .

This feels
incredible . . .

This feels
awesome . . .

This feels
wrong.

I Pull My Hands Out from Under Tessa's Shirt

"Tessa . . ." I say. "Tessa, wait . . .
I'm not sure we should be . . .
I mean,
maybe I shouldn't be doing this . . ."

Tessa blinks at me in confusion
and says, "What's the matter?"
"It's just that I . . . I never told you . . .
I should have told you . . ."

"Told me what?" Tessa says.
"You mean about Sophie?"
My heart stops.
"You *know* about her?!"

"Last night on the phone.
You thought I was *her*, at first.
You sounded so happy when you said her name.
I thought maybe she was your—"

"Sophie's my girlfriend, Tessa.
I've got a girlfriend."
Tessa stares at me,
letting this news sink in.

Then she shrugs
and says, "That's okay, Robin.
Then you and I can just be friends.
Friends with lots and lots and lots

of benefits."

It's Okay with Tessa

But is it okay with *me*?
And what about Sophie?
Oh, man . . . it's hard to think . . .
I'm so mixed up . . .

Tessa leans in and starts kissing me again . . .
God . . . this feels unbelievable . . .
I am so turned on right now . . .
so turned on . . . and so drunk . . .

"Are you . . . I mean . . .
are you sure you don't mind?" I say.
"I'm positive," she says. "I don't need a boyfriend.
I just need someone I can, you know,
sort of practice with."

"You don't need any practice," I say.
"You're great at it already."
And Tessa giggles as I slip my hands
back up underneath her shirt,

letting the vodka
and the kisses
and the soft, soft skin
carry me away.

But a Couple of Minutes Later

Something starts throbbing in my jeans . . .
my cell phone!
My stomach turns inside out—*Sophie?*

I dig it out of my pocket
and check the number.
Whew—it's only my mom.

Not that I exactly wanna talk to *her*, either.
But she'll freak if I don't answer.
I haven't checked in with my parents all day.

"'Sup, Mom?" I say.
"Your dad and I just saw a movie in the Square,
and we want to pick you up before we head home."

No!
This can't be happening.
"Can't you just give me another half hour?"

But Mom says that they're exhausted.
That they need to go home and go to bed—*now.*
And her voice has a real "that's final" sound to it.

So I tell her I'll meet them at the newsstand.
Then I hang up the phone and apologize to Tessa.
She just smiles and says, "Tomorrow?"

"Definitely," I say.
And I kiss her one more time,
before I turn and stumble out the door.

When the Cold Air Hits Me

It sobers me up like a slap across the face.
But even so, if a cop asked me
to walk a straight line right now,
a zigzag would be all I could muster.

I climb into the car.
Will my parents
be able to tell I'm drunk?
Right away my dad starts sniffing the air.

"What's that smell?" he says,
peering at me in the rearview mirror.
Oh, no! Is it the vodka?
"What smell?" I say.

"It's sweet . . ." Mom says.
"Sort of fruity . . ."
"Ohhhh . . ." I say. "*That* smell.
We ate some strawberry Jell-O."

"Jell-O!" Dad says,
pretending to be horrified.
"Those college kids
are such a bad influence on you!"

And both of them crack up.

I'm Not the Type of Person Who Gets Carsick

So how come on the way home,
whenever Dad speeds up
or swerves or steps on the brake,

the stuff in my stomach
feels like it's churning around
inside a blender?

How come every time the tires hit a bump,
it feels like we're slamming into
the side of a mountain?

How come I'm sitting here
covered with a clammy blanket
of cold sweat,

feeling greener
and greener and—
"Dad! Pull over!"

How come
I'm puking my guts out
right now?

Must have been
something
I ate.

I Can't Sleep

So, I'm just lying here on my bed,
staring up at the dim white ceiling
as if it were a movie screen . . .

a movie screen
where I'm projecting my memories
like a film . . .

a film of what happened tonight
when Tessa and I were alone together
in her bedroom . . .

I'm watching myself kissing her,
watching Tessa pulling my hands up
underneath her shirt,

rewinding the film,
to watch *that* part
again and again and again . . .

What Do I Want?

I want it all.

And I should be able to *have* it all,
shouldn't I?

Because Tessa knows about Sophie,
and she doesn't mind.

And Sophie *doesn't* know about Tessa,
so she doesn't mind either.

And, I mean, if no one minds,
then no one's getting hurt, right?

And if no one's
getting hurt,

then there's no reason for me
not to have it all.

Is there?

At Around Noon

My cell phone wakes me.
"Hey, Rockin' Robin," Tessa says.
And her voice sounds so . . .
so intimate and sexy
that just *hearing* it turns me on.

She asks me when I want to get together.
"What's wrong with right *now*?" I say.
Tessa laughs, but she says she's got to finish
writing a paper first.
So we make a plan to meet for dinner.

And it isn't until I hang up the phone
and get out of bed to go to the bathroom,
that I suddenly notice
that my head feels like it's filled with nails.

And that every move I make
sets them jangling and clanging
and crashing together.

So *this*
is what a hangover feels like.

I think

I'm gonna

die.

I'm Getting Ready to Meet Tessa

Checking myself out
in the mirror,

trying not to look
at the portrait I drew of Sophie,

trying to pretend
that she's not up there on my wall,

staring at me
with her eyes full of questions,

questions
I don't want to hear,

questions
I don't know how to answer . . .

I know Sophie *knows* things sometimes.
But I sure hope she doesn't know

about *this*.

Seeing Tessa

I thought maybe it was gonna be weird.
You know—
after everything we did last night.

I thought it might be
a little embarrassing, even,
now that neither one of us is drunk.

But it just seems regular,
like two friends having dinner together,
talking about rock and roll and stuff . . .

until Tessa's knee brushes against mine,
and I let my eyes glance down at her chest,
and suddenly all I can think about is

how much I want to touch her breasts again,
how much I want to get her alone
and tear her sweater off

and just touch them
and touch them
and touch them . . .

Did Tessa Just Read My Mind?

Maybe she *did*.

Because she's pulling on her jacket
and saying, "Come on."

I follow her out of the restaurant
like I've been hypnotized,

follow her down an alley,
behind the building,

into the shadows
of a darkened doorway,

where
without saying a word,

we start kissing and groping
and grinding against each other,

till I can hardly
breathe.

Then a Car Whooshes Past

The light from its high beams
points at us like an accusing finger.
"Let's go," I say, tearing my lips from hers.

We step out of the doorway, out of the alley,
and hurry down Mass Ave together
toward Tessa's dorm,

past the flower shop
and the stationery store,
past the drugstore and the bakery,

and that's when I begin to notice them,
in every window
of every shop—

the red foil hearts,
the cupids with their bows and arrows,
the heart-shaped boxes of chocolate . . .

That's when
I remember
that tomorrow

is Valentine's Day.

And, Right Away, Sophie Pops into My Head

But just thinking about her
makes my chest ache so bad

that I practically feel
like I'm having a heart attack.

And that's
when I realize

that I don't want to go
to Tessa's room with her,

that I *can't* go
to Tessa's room with her.

Because I belong
to *Sophie*,

body
and soul.

I Stop Right Where I Am

And grab Tessa's arm.
"Wait," I say. "Hold on a minute."
She looks at me,
an uncertain smile flickering across her face.
"What is it, Robin?"

"Tessa," I say, searching for the right words.
"Tessa, I really like you . . .
and I *love* making out with you, but—"
"I love making out with you, too," she says.
"So what are we waiting for? Let's go."

"That's what I'm trying to tell you, Tessa.
I can't go with you.
I thought I could do this . . .
this friends-with-benefits thing.
But I don't feel right about it—because of Sophie."

Tessa rakes her fingers through the flames
of her red hair, her face filling with shadows.
"I don't understand, Robin.
How can you not feel right about
doing something that feels so fantastic?"

Then she grabs me
by the lapels of my coat
and gives me a fiery kiss,
throwing her whole self
into trying to get me

to change my mind.

But I Pull Away

Gently, so I won't hurt her feelings.
Then I take hold of both her hands
and say, "I'm sorry, Tessa."

She looks into my eyes
and sees that there's nothing more
she can do.

"Damn . . ." she says, shaking her head.
"Why do you have to be so . . . so honorable?"
She's smiling at me, but her eyes look misty.

I shrug, giving her hands a squeeze.
Then I say, "Ready for a pop quiz?"
"Sure," she says. "Hit me with it."

"Okay:
Which former pair of friends-with-benefits
will stay friends no matter what?"

"Don't go getting all sappy on me," she says,
giving me a playful shove.
But her voice sounds sort of quivery.

She leans in for one more kiss,
a sad, soft, this-is-the-last-time kind of kiss.
Then she breaks away to rush across the street.

I heave a sigh
as I watch her disappear through the gate
into Harvard Yard.

And a second later,
when I turn to walk away,
I glance down the street—

and see *Sophie*!

I Freeze in My Tracks

She's just standing there
looking at me,

less than
half a block away,

just standing there
still as a statue,

in the middle
of the sidewalk,

looking right
at me!

Whoa . . .
How long has she been there?

How much
did she see?

Was she watching
when Tessa

was kissing me?

Suddenly, There's a Tornado in My Chest

Whirling around
in the spot where my heart
used to be.

All I want to do is run away,
run as far away from here
as I can get.

But I force my legs
to carry me toward Sophie
instead.

A second later,
when we're standing
face to face,

and I'm looking into
those heartbreakingly blue
eyes of hers,

I know,
beyond a shadow of a doubt,
that Sophie

saw everything.

Her Hand Flashes Through the Air So Fast

That I don't even see it coming.
The hot sting of it,
the sharp shock of it against my cheek,
stuns me.

"How *could* you, Robin?
How could you *do* that?
I mean, I know we had a fight, but . . ."

My throat's so tight I can barely speak.
"Sophie . . . I'm . . . I'm so sorry . . .
I didn't mean for you to—"
"For me to *what*?" she says.
"Find out that you were *cheating* on me?"

"But, you don't understand. I was—"
"You were kissing her, Robin. I *saw* you."
"Yeah, but I was kissing her *good-bye*, Sophie.
I was telling her it was *over*."

"Over?" she says, her chin trembling.
"Over, as in, like . . . a *relationship*?
How long has this been going *on*, Robin?"
"Only since yesterday. I swear."

"I don't believe you."
"But it's true, Sophie.
I ended it with her because of *you*.
Because I love you."

I reach out to wrap my arms around her,

but she pushes me away—hard.
"Keep your hands *off* me!"

Then she bursts into tears
and runs away from me.
"Sophie!" I shout. "Let me explain!"

But she just keeps right on running.

I Stand Here Watching Her Go

Thinking
if only Tessa and I had gotten here
a few minutes earlier . . .

if only
Sophie had gotten here
a few minutes later . . .

if only
outlaws
still ruled . . .

I Try Everything

I try
calling her cell—
no answer.

I try
calling her house—
no answer.

I try
ringing her doorbell—
no answer.

I even try
tossing pebbles
at her bedroom window—

but she just
switches off
her light.

After Midnight

All I want to do
is escape into sleep.
But every time I close my eyes,
I see Sophie's face,

see the look
that was on it
just before she turned
and ran from me today . . .

and my heart
feels like a stone,
sinking
down
and
down
and
down
through
cold
black
water.

Dad Cracks Open the Door and Looks in on Me

"Robin?" he whispers. "You awake?"
"Yeah."
"I thought you might be."

He comes in and sits down on the edge of my bed.
"You seemed pretty bummed when I
picked you up in the Square tonight . . ." he says,

Aw, for chrissake.
He's not gonna try to get me
to unburden my soul, is he?

But then he says, "I'm feeling kind of blue myself."
Huh? *That's* a switch.
"How come?" I say.

"Well, tomorrow's Valentine's Day,
and I sort of dropped the ball.
You don't happen to have any red paper, do you?

And maybe some glitter or something?
I want to make your mom a valentine.
Girls go gaga over that stuff."

Give me a break—"Girls go gaga over that stuff?"
What kind of loser says things like that?
"Girls go gaga . . . ?" *Gaga . . . ?*

Hey . . . wait a minute . . .
Maybe my dad's actually *onto* something for once—
maybe girls *do* go gaga over that stuff . . .

February Fourteenth

The moon's just the ghost of a smile,
floating on the sky's pink face,
when I finally finish
making everything for Sophie.

But for some strange reason,
I'm not even tired.

I zoom down the hall
to drag Dad out of bed early,
so he can take me to the store
on the way to school.

And for some strange reason,
he doesn't even complain.

I don't tell him my plan,
but when I hop back into the car
and he sees what I've bought,
he high-fives me and wishes me luck.

Like, for some strange reason,
he knows just how much

I'll be needing it.

All Morning Long

I'm sprinting
across campus,
racing against the clock,

to get to each one
of Sophie's classes
before *she* does.

I rush in the door,
ask her teacher where she sits,
hurry to her desk,

and leave
my offerings
on her altar:

a homemade valentine
and a single
rose.

And Every Time

As soon as I've
made my delivery,
I get out of there
as fast as I can.

Because I can't bear to stick around
to watch what happens
when Sophie walks in
and finds what I've left for her.

What if she's tearing up my valentines
without even opening them?
What if she's tossing my roses
into the trash?

What if
nothing I'm doing
is making one bit
of difference?

At Lunchtime

I hurry over to Schultz's room,
so I can catch him
before he heads off to the teachers' lounge.

When I tell him what I want to do,
he smiles at me and says,
"I like a man who thinks big."

Then he reaches into his desk drawer
for his own personal set
of primo French pastels
and says, "Why don't you use these, kiddo?"

So I thank him and set to work on the chalkboard,
drawing an enormous picture of a pig for Sophie.
And inside the heart-shaped speech cloud
over his head I write:

VALENTINE,
I'M SUCH A SWINE.
SWILL YOU BE MINE?

I think
she'll know
who it's from.

When I Tell Schultz I Need to Skip Class

He's cool with it.
So I leave a rose on Sophie's desk
and skulk down the hall to hide out in the library.

Then, when art's over, I go back
to leaving a rose and a valentine for Sophie
in each one of her classes,

always making sure
to be long gone
before she shows up.

And always making sure to avoid
catching even a single glimpse
of her face.

Because I'm afraid
of what I'll see there.
And afraid of what

I *won't*.

4 p.m.

I've been standing here
by the goalpost,
waiting,

just standing here in the knee-knocking cold,
with my eyes trained
on the back door of the building,

picturing Sophie rushing through it,
picturing her running across the field to me
and throwing herself into my arms.

I've been standing here
watching that door
for forty-five minutes now,

while the chill crept into my bones,
and the truth crept into
my heart:

if Sophie
was gonna come to me,
she'd have come to me

by now.

It's Starting to Snow

And the flakes are floating down all around me,
like big frozen tears . . .

I'll freeze to death
if I stay where I am.

But I can't handle the thought
of going home.

Because I can't handle the thought
of walking into my room—

of walking into my room,
looking up at my wall,

and seeing Sophie's portrait
looking back at me.

So I Can't Go Home

But I can't stay here.
Where can I go?
Where?

Suddenly,
the answer hits me:
the Museum of Fine Arts.

If I can just get myself over there
to see *Le Bal à Bougival*
one more time,

if I can just sit down on that wooden bench
and look up at the dancing couple,
like I always used to with Sophie,

I'll somehow feel closer to her,
somehow feel like we're still
connected.

Which I know
is totally corny.
But I don't even care.

It's Not Till I'm Actually *at* the Museum

Not till I'm sprinting up the marble stairway,
toward the impressionist gallery
and *Le Bal à Bougival*,

that I'm finally able
to admit to myself
the *real* reason I've come:

I'm hoping Sophie will be here—
hoping she'll be sitting right there
in front of the painting,

sitting there
waiting for me
on that wooden bench . . .

My feet reach the top of the stairs
and carry me down the hall,
faster and faster, closer and closer . . .

but when I get to the gallery
and hurry through the door,
Sophie's not on the bench—

and the painting's not on the wall!

I Take a Step Back

Reeling from the shock of it—
from the sight of that big blank wall.
The wall where the painting's supposed to be.
Where the painting's *always* been.

Then I notice a little plaque.
It says that *Le Bal à Bougival* is on loan
to a Japanese museum
and won't be back for a year.

I flop down onto the wooden bench,
and, for a long time,
I just sit here,
staring up at that empty space,

while the emptiness inside me
swells and swells,
till it feels like my chest
will burst . . .

The painting's gone.
Sophie's gone.
My one chance for happiness—
gone.

But Then I Hear Footsteps

Footsteps that make me glance
toward the door—
just as *Sophie* walks through it!

When she sees
that the painting's not here,
her eyes fill with tears.

And a second later,
when she shifts her gaze,
she suddenly notices

me.

Her Cheeks Flame Up

Her eyes get wide.

She looks unsteady,
like her knees are weak.

Did she *know* I'd be here?
Is that why she came . . . ?

But the look on her face
says she *didn't* know.

The look on her face
says she wants to hide.

The look on her face
says she's trying to decide

whether to stay
or run away.

I Want to Rush to Her Side

But I'm scared she'll bolt.

I hear myself saying, "Don't worry, Sophie.
It's only on loan . . . It'll be back . . .
It's coming back . . ."

The sound of my voice
seems to help her make up her mind.
Because she starts walking right toward me.

She sits down next to me on the bench,
reaches into her backpack,
and pulls out a sketchbook and a pencil.

Then she opens the book to a blank sheet
and starts crisscrossing it
with straight lines,

making what look like
the empty frames
of a page out of a comic book.

And when all the squares are drawn,
she passes it over
to me.

I Take the Sketchbook from Sophie's Hands

And stare at the first empty frame.
Then I suck in a quick breath
and begin to draw.

It's a picture of Sophie and me
sitting on the wooden bench
in front of the bare museum wall.

And in the thought cloud
floating above my head, I write:
SOMETIMES, I DON'T KNOW *ANYTHING.*

I turn to look
at Sophie's face
and see that she's smiling.

It's a strange kind of smile, sort of crooked,
like she doesn't *want* to be smiling,
only she just can't help it.

And when I reach over,
to cover her hand
with mine—

she doesn't pull away.

Hear how it all started . . .

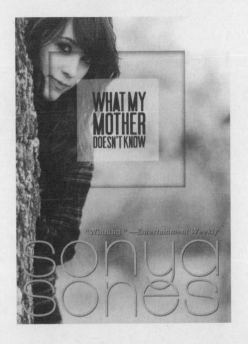

from sophie's point of view.
Turn the page for a peak.

I Don't Get It

I used to think it was so cute
the way Dylan's sneakers always
squeaked when he walked.

I liked teasing him about them.
Called them his squeakers.
Loved being able to hear
him coming a mile away.

When I'd hear that squeak of his
heading in my direction,
my heart would dance right up
into my throat.

I used to feel like I was floating
a few inches above the ground
whenever he was squeaking along
next to me.

But now when I hear those
noisy Nikes of his,
I feel like
I want to scream.

I want to stomp on his toes.
I want to trip him up and run away.
I just don't get it.

HE CALLS HIMSELF CHAZ

I like the ring of it—
chatting with Chaz.
I met him on the Internet last week
and we just seemed to click right away.
No pun intended.

We've been getting together
every night since then at ten o'clock
for these long private talks.
Just the two of us
floating through cyberspace.

There's something so neat
about not even knowing
what he looks like.
Something even neater
about not even caring.

And knowing
that *he* doesn't care
what *I* look like either.
It's a *soul* thing,
with us.

A cybersoul thing.

I made up that word.
Chaz really likes it.

MY MORAL DILEMMA

I ask Rachel and Grace
if they think it's the same thing
as cheating on Dylan
when I chat with Chaz.

Grace says that depends
on who I like talking to more,
the cyberstud (as she calls him)
or Dylan.

Grace says she can't imagine
wanting to talk to another guy
more than her new boyfriend Henry.
On the Net or otherwise.
She says it's a bad sign if
I don't feel that way about Dylan.

But Rachel says one person
can't completely fulfill
anybody's needs a hundred percent
and it's not as if
I'm actually *dating* Chaz,
so she doesn't see anything wrong with it.

I love that girl.

CYBER SOUL MATE

It's almost ten o'clock.
I can hardly wait
to see his voice.

HIS WORDS POP ONTO MY SCREEN:

"So tell me about your day.
I want to know everything that happened
from the minute you woke up this morning
to right now."

I don't think anyone's
ever
been this interested in me before.
Not even *me*.

As I place my fingers
to the keys
and begin,
my heart does the happy chatroom dance.

MORE OR LESS

If Dylan and I had met
by chatting on the Net
in a room in cyberspace
instead of face to face
and I hadn't seen his lips
or the way he moves his hips
when he does that sexy dance
and I hadn't had a chance
to look into his eyes
or be dazzled by their size
and all that I had seen
were his letters on my screen,
then I might as well confess:
I think I would have liked him

less.

Double Date

All Grace has to do is smile at him
and Henry forgets what he's saying
right in the middle of his sentence.

And when he *can complete a thought,*
Grace acts like it's just about
the funniest thing she's ever heard.

Henry keeps wrapping
the little curl at the nape of her neck
around his finger,

and he hasn't let go of her hand once,
even to scratch,
since we've been here,

which seems like hours
even though it's probably only been
twenty minutes.

I don't know how
they're going to manage it
when the food comes.

Dylan and I are just sitting here
across from them in the booth,
trying to make small talk.

Our thighs
aren't even touching
on the seat.

At the Movies

I'm sitting between Henry and Dylan.
Dylan's holding my hand,
but I can tell he isn't *feeling* it.

He's actually watching the movie.
I mean *really* watching it,
like it doesn't even matter that I'm here.

And the saddest part is
that I don't care.
I'd almost rather snuggle up to Henry.

But he's too busy holding hands
(and everything else)
with Grace.

WALKING HOME

The light changes
and Dylan and I head across the street,
arm in arm.

That's when it happens:
I notice our reflection in
the window of Starbucks
and I get this weird feeling
that something isn't quite right.
Only I can't put my finger on it.

Then it hits me:
what's wrong is that it looks like
I'm *taller* than Dylan,
which is totally bizarre
because I'm wearing my flattest shoes
and I know for a fact
that he's taller than me.

At least he *was* taller
six weeks ago
when we first started
going out together.

I've heard of people
outgrowing relationships,
but *this* is ridiculous.

GOOD NIGHT

We're standing under the porch light,
face to face,
leaning our foreheads together.

He's playing with my fingers,
whispering something
about what a great time he had tonight.

And all I can think about
is that his hands look smaller than mine,
like the hands of a little boy.

Q AND A WITH CHAZ

"Do you have a boyfriend?"
"Yes."

"Do you have a girlfriend?"
"Yes."

"Who is she?"
"You."

Me?!

"Yikes."
"Yeah."

Ally Ryan is about to discover that
it turns out you can go home again,
but it will pretty much suck.

She's *So* Dead to Us

kieran scott

*The first book in a new series abou
losing it all and being better off
from author Kieran Scot.*

what if one summer *everything* changed?
would *you* be ready?

"THIS BOOK HAS WHAT EVERY GIRL WANTS IN A SUMMER."
—Sarah Dessen, author of *Just Listen* and *Lock and Key*

the summer
i turned *pretty*

JENNY HAN
AUTHOR OF *SHUG*